"Men!"

The word was out of her mouth before she could stop it. "No," Harriet corrected herself, "the real problem is men like you."

"Men like me?" Dexter asked. "And what type of man is that?"

That was a pretty colossal question! Harriet made a face, but said nothing. Her answer was burning a hole in her tongue, but she had to be discreet. After all, he was her employer.

"Go on. You can tell me."

"I'd really rather not."

"Are you afraid you might offend me?"

She would love to offend him, but she had no desire to lose her job! Her opinion of Dexter Ross was that he was arrogant and cold-hearted and incapable of caring for anyone but himself. She smiled a careful smile. "I think we ought to change th...

Stephanie Howard is a British author whose two ambitions since childhood were to see the world and to write. Her first venture became a four-year stay in Italy, learning the language and supporting herself by writing short stories. Then her sensible side brought her back to London to study Social Administrations at the London School of Economics. She has held various editorial posts at magazines such as *Reader's Digest*, *Vanity Fair* and *Women's Own*.

Books by Stephanie Howard

THE PHARAOH'S KISS
Stephanie Howard

Harlequin Books

TORONTO • NEW YORK • LONDON
AMSTERDAM • PARIS • SYDNEY • HAMBURG
STOCKHOLM • ATHENS • TOKYO • MILAN
MADRID • WARSAW • BUDAPEST • AUCKLAND

ISBN 0-373-17204-4

THE PHARAOH'S KISS

CHAPTER ONE

HARRIET felt her heart sink as she stood by the desk and watched the receptionist tick off her name.

'Are all these other names,' she enquired, nodding at the appointments book, 'applicants for the same job I'm being interviewed for?'

The receptionist smiled brightly and nodded her head. 'Mr Ross had a terrific response to his ad. He's been interviewing all morning, and he'll be interviewing all afternoon. But you're the last one he'll be seeing before lunch.'

'I see.' Harriet seated herself on one of the chairs that lined the walls of the sumptuous Mayfair office and told herself that this was no more than she ought to have expected. The newspaper ad had been nothing if not enticing. She was bound to be just one among scores of eager applicants.

She shook back her shoulder-length copper-brown hair and recalled the moment when her eyes had alighted on the ad.

Assistant to archæologist required immediately for four weeks' work in Egypt. Exceptionally generous rate of pay.

A light had instantly switched on inside her head. This is it! she'd thought excitedly. This is the solution to all my problems!

But perhaps, she reflected now, she'd been a little optimistic in her assumption that the job would be

5

hers for the taking. It looked as though she was up against some stiff opposition!

The door to what was evidently Ross's office opened suddenly with a click. A pretty blonde girl stepped out, smiling broadly, clearly pleased with the way her interview had gone. And Harriet felt another plummet of anxiety. She needed this job desperately. How would she manage if she didn't get it?

There was a pause as the blonde girl strode towards the exit, then the phone on the receptionist's desk gave a quick, sharp buzz.

The receptionist smiled across at Harriet. 'You may go in now, Miss Kaye. Mr Ross is ready to see you.'

And I'm ready to see him. Harriet drew a deep breath as she rose from her chair and, squaring her shoulders, headed for the door to Ross's office. And suddenly all her anxiety seemed to slip away from her. I need this job, she told herself fiercely, and I'm going to do everything in my power to get it!

Just inside the doorway, she paused for an instant—a slim, elegant figure in a cream cotton suit, her blue eyes narrowing in momentary bewilderment. The big, sunlit room appeared to be empty. The desk by the window stood vast and unoccupied. Perhaps, she wondered in bafflement, I'm in the wrong place.

Then a deep voice spoke. 'Please take a seat. I'll be with you in a moment.'

Harriet swung round to face the spot where the voice had come from and found herself looking into a dark-eyed face, the like of which she had never looked into before.

He was standing by an imposing, glass-fronted bookcase at the opposite end of the room from the desk. A tall, broad-shouldered figure in an expensively tailored suit, hair as black as jet, features carved from granite. In one hand he held a book which he appeared to be consulting.

In fact, as Harriet turned to look at him, he raised his eyes for only an instant. But that brief, flickering instant was more than long enough to allow her to register, with an inward shiver, the power and vitality that sprang from his face. It was almost a relief when his eyes dropped away again.

Harriet turned, oddly shaken by this unexpected encounter, and crossed the room to do as he had bade her, seating herself on one of the leather-backed chairs that were arranged on the nearside of the huge mahogany desk.

Then she smiled to herself as a sudden thought occurred to her. In his ad this man had described himself as an archaeologist, an amiable breed she associated in her mind with dishevelled corduroys and shaggy grey beards. She'd been expecting a fatherly-looking figure in his fifties. This man was two decades younger and definitely not at all fatherly. No wonder she'd felt a trifle nonplussed at the sight of him!

There was the sound of footsteps approaching her across the carpet. And, again, Harriet felt a shiver go through her. He had this knack, she found herself observing with a leap of irritation, to overpower one simply with the force of his presence.

But he would not overpower her. She wasn't that impressionable. She raised cool blue eyes to his as he paused at her side and spoke.

'Allow me to introduce myself. I'm Dexter Ross.' He extended one hand. 'And you, I believe, are Miss Harriet Kaye?'

'That is correct.' Harriet accepted his proffered hand. His grip was cool and firm and brief.

'And you are here, presumably, because you believe yourself qualified to accompany me as my assistant on my expedition to Egypt?' There was an edge to his tone, as he delivered the query, that suggested he found her assumption presumptuous.

Harriet looked into his face, as he continued to stand over her, resisting the power of those midnight-dark eyes. Not power, she corrected herself. Undiluted arrogance. Dexter Ross was male arrogance on legs.

She said, 'Your ad, if I may say so, was somewhat vague. It failed to specify precisely the qualifications you're looking for. But I have numerous skills, I learn fast and I'm adaptable. I thought there was a fair chance I might fit the bill.'

Dexter Ross rode the rebuke in her tone with a sudden smile. He allowed his eyes to flicker unhurriedly over her. 'I have no doubt you speak the truth... at least in regard to your numerous skills.' As he continued to smile and watch her, she caught a glimpse of perfect teeth. 'But are they the skills I'm looking for in the context of personal assistant? That is what we have to find out.'

There was something about his scrutiny that caused her skin to tingle. It was as though he had reached out and touched her with a finger.

Harriet felt her breath catch. That sense of intimacy had been unexpected. And totally unwelcome, she told herself briskly.

'Then let's find out. After all, that's what I'm here for.' With careful composure she shook back her hair. 'I suggest we get on with the interview.'

'My thoughts precisely.' He had stepped away from her and was moving round the desk to the button-back chair that stood behind it. His movements, Harriet observed as he lowered himself into it, were easy and graceful, like the movements of an athlete. At least there was this much to be said for him... He was a pleasure to the eye!

Dexter Ross leaned back in the button-back chair and flicked a glance across the desk at her. 'So, tell me, Miss Harriet Kaye, what reasons do you have for believing that you may be the assistant I'm looking for?'

Harriet narrowed her eyes. 'I might be able to answer that better if you were to tell me the particular attributes you're looking for.'

'You mean besides multiple, undefined skills, an ability to learn fast and adaptability?' He smiled again—a slow, amused smile. But behind the smile was tempered steel. Harriet sensed it sharply. This man's heart was made of nails.

She said, aware of a growing antipathy, 'Tell me what you're looking for and I'll tell you if I can supply it.'

'No, let's begin with you.'

His eyes surveyed her. And now that they were more or less on a level with her own Harriet could see the startling beauty of those eyes. They were not particularly large, but spaced wide apart, and they were as deep and black as pools of treacle. They dominated his face with its clean, sculpted lines, strong nose, high cheekbones and curved, sensuous mouth. They were eyes it felt almost sinful to look too deeply into.

What a foolish notion! Harriet rejected it quickly. 'So, what do you wish to know about me?' she enquired levelly.

'You could start by telling me what you normally do for a living. That might offer me some clues as to your suitability.'

'I'm a dancer.' As one straight, sweeping jet-black eyebrow lifted and a look of caustic amusement touched the dark eyes, she hurried on, 'Or, more accurately, I run my own school of dancing. I've been running it now for two and a half years.'

'A dancer?' He made no attempt to disguise his mirth. A low, dismissive laugh issued from his lips. 'And what use, Miss Harriet Kaye, could a dancer possibly be to me? I'm planning to go on an archaeological expedition. I'm not planning to learn to tango on top of the pyramids.'

'It never crossed my mind you were.' His cutting humour irked her. Harriet felt her fists clench angrily in her lap. And her tone was only just on the right side of politeness—after all, she badly needed this job!—as she pointed out to him, 'As a dancer, I'm fit and used to physical exertion. After all, I spend most of my working day exercising my body.'

'In forty-plus-degree heat? In the middle of the desert? Are you also used to that, Miss Harriet Kaye?'

Forty degrees plus, Harriet calculated quickly, was well up over a hundred degrees Fahrenheit.

'Sometimes even higher. Sometimes it can touch fifty.' Seeing her pause, he took pleasure in deliberately stoking what he perceived to be her alarm. 'No doubt you also experience these sorts of temperatures every day of your working life?'

'No, not in Sittingbourne. That would be most unusual.' Harriet allowed herself a quick, sarcastic smile. 'It would be a trifle foolish of me to make such claims.'

He paused and smiled fleetingly. 'And you, I take it, do not consider yourself to be foolish?'

It was a rhetorical question that really required no answer. But it caught Harriet unawares. She felt her heart squeeze painfully and a revealing flicker of emotion touched her eyes. Foolishness, as she had learned recently, was not a frailty she was exempt from. It was foolishness that had brought about her current predicament.

She said, a little too honestly, 'I suppose I'm no more foolish than the next person.'

Dexter had picked up her reaction and had read between the lines. For a moment the dark eyes regarded her narrowly. But, to Harriet's relief, he did not pursue the subject. Instead, he reached out to pick up the gold paper-knife that lay on the blotter on his desk.

'So, continue,' he commanded her. 'Apart from physical fitness, what other attributes do you have to offer?'

Harriet sighed. 'It really would make things easier if you were to tell me the particular attributes you're looking for. How can I tell you what I have to offer when I don't even know what the job entails?'

'I'll tell you later what the job entails. In the meantime I simply want you to tell me about yourself—without being tempted to add and elaborate in order to fit in with my requirements.' Before she could protest, he raised one hand to silence her. 'Not that I believe for one minute that you would be so foolish. After all, as we have established, foolishness is not one of your weaknesses...'

Harriet sighed inwardly. He had definitely picked that slip up, and she had given herself away so easily! And now, she sensed, he would take great pleasure in using her momentary slip against her. When would she learn to be just a tiny bit more devious?

But guile would never be one of Harriet's strengths—no more than would the ability to hide her feelings. Every emotion that touched her was destined to be revealed in her eyes.

But the emotion that was reflected there now was determination. She would not allow herself to be undermined by Dexter Ross and his subtle, half-spoken observations. She would do what she had come here for—namely, to make sure she got the job! And in the process she would reveal nothing of her own unhappy circumstances. They were none of his business and she would keep them to herself!

She watched for a moment as he toyed with the paper-knife, its gold sheen flashing between his long tanned fingers. There was something discreetly sensual, yet oddly threatening about his movements. And again that sense that he was as hard as the metal between his fingers forged itself, like a warning, on to her brain.

Then she raised her eyes to his. 'Very well, Mr Ross. I'll do my best to give you a brief run-down of my capabilities . . .'

Dexter Ross said nothing. Black eyes watching her, he waited.

Harriet drew herself up to her full height in her seat. She cleared her throat quickly. 'As I told you,' she began, 'I run my own business, a dancing school in Sittingbourne. These days, because business is doing so well, I employ a part-time secretary as well as a couple of other teachers. With so many classes to run I just don't have time to manage the administrative side of things on my own any more.'

She crossed her slender legs, adjusting the hem of her skirt. 'But, in the beginning, I used to do everything myself. Making appointments, keeping records, invoices, everything. I know how to use a computer, a fax machine . . . all modern office equipment, in fact. I've even been involved in making promotional videos, I've dealt with advertising and done several media interviews.'

She paused, rather pleased with this list of achievements. By any standards, it wasn't bad for a twenty-four-year-old girl. 'As I told you, I can turn my hand to most things. And I'm a very good organiser. I'm good at getting things done.'

'Most impressive.' Dexter Ross continued to study her face. Then he smiled and slowly raised his straight black eyebrows, and there was no more warmth in his smile than in the paper-knife in his hand. He allowed a moment of silence to flow between them. Its purpose, Harriet guessed, was to unnerve her a little.

'So, why,' he put to her, 'with so many skills at your disposal, and with a business of your own, which you assure me is flourishing, are you the least bit interested in applying for the position as my temporary assistant?'

Harriet was aware of a stab of acute discomfort. Before her eyes for an instant flickered an image of Tom. A dart of pain and betrayal went shooting through her. She glanced away quickly, lest Ross read it in her eyes. That black gaze, as she had already learned, picked up everything.

Then she raised her eyes again. She would not lie to him, but neither would she disclose the heartbreaking truth. 'I'm not working at the moment. The school is closed for a month. I'm having some essential building repairs done.'

'In that case, wouldn't it be wiser for you to stay and supervise things? It's very trusting of you to go off and leave the workmen to themselves.'

Harriet cleared her throat. 'My secretary will look after things. There's no need for me to stay.'

'I see.' There was another unnerving silence. The gold paper-knife flashed between the deeply tanned fingers. 'I still find it a little odd that someone in your position should have any interest in applying for the job I advertised.' He paused. She was obviously expected to explain herself.

Harriet, in fact, had anticipated this demand. More in control of herself now, she told him frankly, 'What motivated me primarily was the money. Your ad promised, if I recall correctly, an extremely generous rate of pay.'

'You recall correctly.' As he continued to regard her, he quoted a figure that was indeed most generous. She had been right—this job would solve her problems!

Then he added, 'But why should you find that so enticing when you are the owner of a thriving, flourishing business?'

Harriet swallowed, biting back another surge of raw emotion. 'Repairs always cost more than you think,' she answered. It was a misleading answer, but it was scarcely a lie! 'A bit of extra money always comes in useful.'

'Indeed it does.' His eyes were closely watching her. She could sense he knew there was something she was hiding. 'So, it was in search of a bit of extra money that you came across my ad in the situations vacant column?'

Harriet nodded. 'Yes.' If only, she was thinking, he would let go of this deeply distressing subject.

'You must have been quite desperate for a bit of extra money. Most temporary jobs don't pay very much.'

'No, they don't.' Harriet shifted her gaze as she said it. Her heart felt as tight as a drum in her chest.

'Hardly worth the effort of pursuing, I would have thought, for a girl with her own prosperous, thriving business.'

Every syllable was like a knife driving into her heart. Harriet's gaze shifted again, her discomfort obvious. 'Every little helps,' was all she could think of by way of an answer.

Dexter sat back in his chair and, his eyes never leaving her, rolled the gold paper-knife between the palms of his hands. 'Of course,' he observed, his tone flat, oddly menacing, 'perhaps you have another reason for wishing to spend a month in Egypt?'

'Like what, for example?'

'How would I know? It's clearly some reason you prefer to keep to yourself.'

What was he suggesting? Harriet narrowed her blue eyes at him. 'Like maybe I'm on the run from the police, for example?' Her tone was suddenly taut with irritation. This interview was turning into an inquisition. 'I can assure you, Mr Ross, I'm not a refugee from the law.'

'That thought had not occurred to me.' His gaze never flickered. 'But it is still a mystery to me why you should be so keen to get this job.'

'Perhaps I want to see Egypt.'

'That would be forgivable.' A smile that seemed almost genuine flickered momentarily across his face. 'Egypt is a fascinating and beautiful country.'

Harriet sensed a slight thaw. Gratefully, she took advantage. 'The thought of combining a trip to Egypt with the chance to make a bit of extra money ... I suppose that's what attracted me to the ad.'

'A trip to Egypt? You make it sound like a holiday.' His voice was sheet ice, obliterating that brief thaw. 'What I'm offering is not some paid holiday, Miss Kaye. What I'm offering is hard work, and plenty of it.'

'All the better! I'm not looking for a holiday!' Instantly, Harriet rushed to put him right. He had deliberately misunderstood her. Then she added with feeling—perhaps a little more feeling than she'd intended—'Hard work and plenty of it is precisely what I'm looking for!'

'Is that so? How very interesting.' As the dark eyes surveyed her, Harriet sensed keenly that, unwittingly, she had betrayed herself again. And that suspicion was strengthened as Dexter Ross continued, 'One who runs her own flourishing, thriving business, I would imagine, spends most of her time working hard. I'd have expected in the circumstances that you'd be grateful for a rest.'

He held her eyes for one deeply penetrating moment. 'But then, hard work is known to be a most effective therapy...for those who are running away...though not from the law...'

Harriet was glad that at that moment one of the phones on his desk rang. His suggestion was uncomfortably close to the truth. Hard work, it had occurred to her also, was an excellent therapy. But that was not something she wished to discuss with him.

As he spoke into the phone, he had swivelled his chair away from her, so that now she was presented with his dark aquiline profile. Harriet regarded it with dislike. Rarely in her life had she been afflicted with so intense a sense of antipathy for someone. An antipathy that all too clearly was returned with interest. This interview, she sensed strongly, with a sense of despair and inevitability, was destined to be a complete and utter waste of time.

She detached her eyes from the hostile dark profile. Looking at him simply made her blood churn. And she must overcome her antipathy. She must make a good impression. Against all the odds she must somehow win this job.

Harriet took a calming breath, sat back in her seat and, to avoid looking at Ross, turned to glance round the room. And for the first time she noticed in the glass cases that lined the walls what appeared to be a collection of priceless Egyptian artefacts.

Masks inlaid with gold and lapis lazuli, jewel-studded collars fit for a pharaoh, exquisitely carved cats with gold earrings in their ears. Her eyes widened at the beauty of it all. She longed to take a closer look.

'Do you like them?'

Harriet spun round, surprised to find him watching her. She had been unaware that he had ended his phone conversation. She wondered how long he had been sitting there spying on her.

'They're wonderful,' she told him frankly, annoyed that her words clearly pleased him. 'I had no idea such treasures existed in private collections.'

'Very few do.'

'They ought to be in a museum.' There was a note of censure in her tone. 'In my opinion, treasures like these ought to be kept in a public place where anyone who cares to can enjoy them.'

'I disagree. I prefer to enjoy them in private. It gives me great pleasure to know I have them all to myself.'

What a selfish remark! And not just selfish—faintly shocking. Recklessly, making no effort to disguise her disapproval, Harriet told him, 'Quite frankly, I'm surprised that the Egyptian government allows such treasures to be taken out of the country. I would say they belong in Egypt. In a museum.'

'Would you?'

'Yes, I would.' As he simply smiled across at her, quite unaffected by her censure, Harriet couldn't resist adding, 'Do the Egyptians know you've got them? It seems astonishing to me that they'd part voluntarily with such treasures.'

'Are you suggesting that I might be some kind of tomb robber?' Dexter picked up the gold paper-knife that he had earlier laid aside, and toyed with it, his dark eyes watching her with amusement. 'Are you suggesting that I stole them and then smuggled them out of the country?'

Harriet delivered him a long look. Perhaps you did, she was thinking. For there was something about him that made her sense very strongly that Dexter Ross would be capable of almost anything.

She said carefully, 'I'm not suggesting anything.' It would be unwise, she was thinking, in spite of her suspicions, to accuse him to his face of being a thief! Still, she couldn't resist adding, looking around her, 'It would, of course, help to explain all this. I imagine there are very few archaeologists around who can afford an office in the middle of Mayfair.'

'I tend to agree with you. There must be very few indeed.' Dexter smiled enigmatically, making it very clear that he had no intention of elaborating further on the subject.

There was a silence, Dexter watching her, knowing she was curious, enjoying giving nothing away.

Harriet, sensing his enjoyment, assumed an air of indifference. 'But how you acquired them, quite frankly, is of no great interest to me. The only point I was trying to make was that in my opinion your collection of antiquities ought to be in a public museum.'

The gold of the paper-knife glinted smugly, reflecting the profoundly smug look in the dark eyes. 'Well, on that point I'm afraid we must agree to differ. The collection is here. And the collection is mine. Mine to enjoy in privacy whenever the mood takes me.'

He paused, holding her eyes, before adding with a smile that seemed to Harriet deliberately provocative, 'And that is a state of affairs that pleases me immensely.'

Yes, Harriet could see that. She looked at him with understanding. He's a taker, she thought. Another shameless taker. A breed I seem to have a knack of tripping over!

The thought caused a flicker of tension inside her. A picture of Tom with his earnest grey eyes and soft, pleading tongue rose up momentarily in her mind, and with it that familiar stabbing sense of betrayal.

She banished it instantly, with impatience at herself, but not before the sharp eyes of the man who sat watching her had picked up her momentary, fleeting reaction.

He said, strong tanned fingers toying idly with the paper-knife, 'Is there something on your mind? Is there something troubling you?'

'Something on my mind?' Harriet quickly shook her head. 'All that's on my mind is proceeding with this interview.' She smiled, disguising how exposed and threatened she felt by this man's uncanny ability to see beneath her skin. 'We seem to have strayed a little from the point.'

'The point?'

'The point of my being here.' She held her smile in place. 'We seem to have got a little side-tracked.'

'You think so?' He held the paper-knife poised between his index fingers. Harriet found herself wishing it might slip and pierce his flesh. Almost as though he knew that, he unexpectedly released his hold on it, then, with a swift, precise movement, caught it in his hand.

Smiling, he told her, 'I'm afraid I can't agree. I don't think we've been side-tracked in the slightest. On the contrary, the interview is proceeding most satisfactorily. What I have learned about you so far I'm sure will prove most helpful when it comes to finally deciding your suitability for the job.'

Harriet found this pronouncement less than encouraging. Hadn't she sensed that most of what he had learned about her was not to his liking?

But, before she could say anything, he was putting to her, 'But there must be some questions you'd like to ask me?' He leaned back in his seat and tossed down the paper-knife, the gesture subtly underlining this sudden change of tack. 'Feel free,' he invited. 'Fire away.' As he spoke, he stretched his long legs out under the desk.

Harriet drew her own crossed legs back under her chair. It was a reflex action that struck her as odd and silly. Stiffly self-protective. A trifle spinsterish.

Deliberately, she relaxed them as she responded, 'The main question I would like answered is the one I've already asked you. What exactly does the job entail? So far you haven't been very forthcoming about that.'

'Perhaps because the job doesn't fall into any particularly clear category. It's made up of all sorts of odd bits and pieces...'

He was being deliberately evasive because he knew it annoyed her. Harriet counted up to ten. 'What sorts of bits and pieces?'

Dexter smiled, evidently finding her impatience amusing. 'Well, there's a bit of secretarial work involved. I need someone to take notes for me when I'm working... Generally, I dictate into a tape recorder. All my assistant has to do is take charge of the tape recorder, then type up the notes at the end of each day.'

That sounded simple enough. Harriet felt her spirits lift. She demanded, with renewed optimism, 'That would be no problem. What else?'

'On the secretarial side, the usual sort of stuff. Sending faxes, making appointments, writing letters, handling phone calls—and making sure I'm where I'm supposed to be at any given time.'

That last requirement was the only one that Harriet could see as problematic. Trying to organise Dexter Ross, she sensed, would be no picnic. But she refused to let that thought dispirit her.

She said, 'And is that it on the secretarial side?'

Dexter shrugged. 'More or less. Do you feel equipped to handle it?'

'With no problem at all. As I've already told you, I have experience in all sorts of office and secretarial work.'

'Indeed you did.' The black eyes were laughing at her. 'But then so has every other applicant I've seen so far. And I expect the others I'll be seeing this afternoon to be similarly well-qualified.'

Harriet flinched a little inwardly. She had briefly forgotten the stiffness of the opposition she was up against. But her gaze was steady as she met that of Dexter Ross. 'So, what else does the job involve besides the secretarial stuff you've outlined?'

He did not answer immediately. He let his gaze drift over her, causing her skin to tingle again strangely and her blood to jump in her veins. He's trying to psych me, she thought irritably, and he's almost succeeding.

Then at last, laying his arms along the arms of his chair, his fingers cupping the carved ends, he spoke. 'The secretarial side of things, let me make it plain, is the easy part. I could walk out on to the street right this minute and find a dozen girls who fitted the bill.' He sat forward in his seat and delivered her a long look. 'It's the non-secretarial side of things that requires rather particular attributes . . .'

'For example?'

'For example . . .' The black eyes drove into her. 'For example, do you suffer from claustrophobia, Miss Kaye?'

The question was unexpected. 'No, I don't.' Harriet blinked.

'Do you know that for sure? Has your claim ever been tested? Have you ever, for example, been trapped in a lift?'

'As a matter of fact, I have.' She vaguely remembered it. 'It didn't upset me particularly. I'm definitely not claustrophobic.' She was about to ask what claustrophobia had to do with anything, but before she could he was firing more questions at her.

'How do you cope in conditions of intense heat? How would you bear up to spending long hours out in the desert, trekking about across the sand-dunes?'

Harriet, quite frankly, had no idea. 'I can't tell you,' she answered honestly. 'The greatest heat I've ever experienced was a couple of times on holiday in Crete. I found I adjusted OK after a couple of days. I'm not particularly fair-skinned. I can cope with the sun. But I've never been anywhere near a desert.'

She paused for an instant. 'However, I imagine in such circumstances one simply has to use one's common sense—drink rather a lot and look for whatever shade one can find.'

Dexter Ross smiled at that. 'Yes, common sense always helps.'

'And, in addition to common sense, I have a dancer's physical stamina. You won't find many young women who are quite as fit as I am.'

Again the dark eyes swept over her. A smile touched his lips. 'From what I can see, I have no argument with that.'

'Which all adds up,' Harriet added quickly, scarcely able to believe his suddenly more positive attitude, 'to a pretty strong argument in my favour.'

'On the face of it, it would appear so.' He held her gaze. 'However... you still haven't answered one important question...'

'And what question is that?' Harriet leaned forward in her seat, hope and apprehension mingled in her face.

He looked deep into her eyes. 'The question is this... What are you running away from, Miss

Harriet Kaye? Why are you so desperate to get this job?'

'I told you I need the money.'

'And I accept that that's part of it. But there's more.' His eyes pierced her. 'What are you running away from?'

'Nothing! It's personal! I don't have to answer that!' He had probed too deeply, come too close to her private sorrow, just when she had believed she was safe from his prying. And now, wrong-footed, once more she had revealed herself.

She said again, defensively, 'It's nothing to do with you. It's personal.'

'Personal?'

'Yes, personal. Extremely personal.'

Dexter sat back in his seat. 'So, it's as I suspected.' He sighed. 'There's some man in the middle of all this.'

Harriet felt herself flush. She pursed her lips and said nothing. Suddenly she found herself hating Dexter Ross.

He continued, immune to the message in her eyes, 'It would appear that some man has recently broken your heart. That's what you're running away from. A broken romance.'

It was too close to the truth for Harriet to deny it. But she had to defend herself. 'What has any of this to do with the job?'

'A great deal, I'm afraid.' He surveyed her without compassion. 'One thing I have absolutely no need of is some lovesick girl tagging along with me, pretending she's there to do a job of work when all the time her mind is somewhere else.'

He half rose from his chair. 'We're wasting each other's time. I wouldn't even dream of entertaining such a nonsense.'

'But that's not the way it would be!' Harriet looked up at him in horror. A moment ago she'd thought the job was almost hers. And now, suddenly, all hope had vanished into thin air. 'You're wrong!' she insisted. 'It's not that way at all!'

'You mean there's no man?'

Harriet swallowed, but could not answer.

'No broken heart?'

She glanced away, unable to look at him.

'You're wrong,' she murmured. 'You're judging me unfairly. I can do the job. You'll find no one better.'

He had risen fully from his chair now. Harriet could feel him standing over her. He said, 'You may be able to fool yourself, but I'm afraid, Miss Kaye, you can't fool me. As I see it, you are manifestly unfit for the job. For the reasons I have just stated.'

'You're wrong.' It was a final, futile protest, spoken to herself as much as to him. Then, when he did not answer, Harriet rose to her feet slowly, knowing she was beaten, angry at the injustice of it, and, without another word, stepped away from her chair.

Dexter led her to the door and pulled it open. 'I hope you find something . . .' He paused an instant and added in a tone edged with mocking sympathy, 'Something more suited to your current fragile frame of mind.'

That brought Harriet up short. The very last thing she needed was the sympathy of this arrogant, hateful man. This arrogant, hateful man, whom, if she considered it sensibly, the thought of working alongside was frankly unbearable.

She turned to look at him. 'I think you've made the right decision—though not because of the reasons you've given me,' she told him.

As the dark eyes widened curiously, she added tightly, 'You and I could never have worked together, Mr Ross. Even if you'd offered me the job, it would have been a mistake for me to take it. I suspect you've done us both a favour.'

Then with head held high, all her dignity intact, triumphantly aware of the surprised dark eyes that followed her, Harriet turned and walked quickly through the door.

CHAPTER TWO

So, THAT was it. No job. No money. And no way she could see of paying the builders' bills.

Despondently, Harriet stared out of the carriage window as the train took her south from London to Sittingbourne, wishing she had never seen Dexter Ross's wretched ad, never gone to the interview, and never made such a hash of it.

For, in spite of that face-saving gesture of bravado when she had told him he had done them both a favour by turning her down so categorically for the job, the truth was that, if he had offered it, she would have grabbed it with both hands. Working with Dexter Ross would undoubtedly have been a nightmare, but the money he was offering was the answer to her prayers.

But she'd blown her chance. It had been there within her grasp—for she was right for the job, she was quite convinced of that—and he'd snatched it away from her, totally unfairly. And the only one she had to blame was herself.

Harriet breathed deeply and tried to drag herself out of her despondency. Perhaps, if she kept looking, she would find something else—though not, she knew for certain, with the salary Ross had been offering. The best she could hope for was some poorly paid position that would do little more than take the edge off her predicament.

She would have to resort to a loan—if her bank manager would allow it, and there was a more than even chance that he would not, for she was already weighed down at every corner with loans and overdrafts and mortgage repayments.

Harriet sighed. That made her sound like a hopeless businesswoman, as though her finances were in a state of total chaos. And they weren't. Or, rather, they hadn't been. In fact, quite the opposite. She sighed again. It was Tom she had to thank for this mess.

But thinking of Tom only made her feel worse. Her heart weighed inside her like a lump of cold lead. He used me, she thought, anger biting at her misery. And I should have known. I should have seen through him.

At Sittingbourne station Harriet picked up her car and drove the half-dozen miles to the little cottage where she lived. She parked outside and sat for a moment, gloomily contemplating her future. If there was no way of laying hands on the money, perhaps she would have to consider selling her little cottage and finding herself a smaller, cheaper flat.

She would hate to do it, but what choice would she have? The repairs to the dancing school were absolutely essential. She wouldn't be able to reopen next term if they weren't done.

The very thought made her shiver. The school was her livelihood. Her livelihood and her passion. And she had worked so hard to build it up. It would be more than she could bear if she were to lose the school.

Sunk in her misery, Harriet almost didn't hear the shrill of the telephone ringing in the hall. It was only as she stepped despondently out on to the pavement that suddenly, belatedly, she became aware of it.

As her heart leapt inside her, she began to hurry up the path, telling herself it was probably nothing important, yet suddenly frantic to reach the phone before it stopped ringing.

She burst through the front door and snatched up the receiver. 'Hello?' Her hand was shaking as she clamped it to her ear.

He took a moment to answer. He had been about to hang up. But then he spoke and suddenly Harriet's heart was flying in her chest.

'This is Dexter Ross. You've got the job. We leave for Egypt on Monday morning.'

'Here's your passport, with your Egyptian visa. There were no problems, I'm pleased to say. Everything's in order.'

They were sitting on the huge butter-soft hide sofa that dominated the sitting-room of Ross's Mayfair penthouse, Harriet at one end and Dexter at the other, sorting out the details of tomorrow's flight to Egypt.

Harriet took her passport and laid it beside her, trying to douse the grin she knew was spread across her face. Everything had happened so fast since that miraculous phone call that had so taken her by surprise just four short days ago. She could barely believe this stroke of good fortune that had come along and saved her when she had already abandoned hope. She had scarcely stopped smiling since it had happened.

'And here's some reading material for the flight.'
Dexter leaned and picked up the heavy-looking
folder that was lying on the glass-topped table
nearby. He tossed it across the sofa to Harriet. 'A
bit of background information,' he told her. 'Just
so you know what the expedition's all about.'

Harriet glanced down at the folder, smiling and
undaunted. 'I look forward to reading it,' she told
him with enthusiasm.

'I'm afraid I expect you to do more than just
read it. I expect you to study it with close attention.
I expect you to know, accurately and in detail,
what's in that folder by the time we touch down in
Luxor.'

Harriet met the steely gaze. Damned martinet!
she was thinking. Even here at home in the privacy
of his own apartment he remained as hard-edged
and arrogant as he had been at their first meeting!

He was dressed now in an open-necked shirt and
light trousers that superficially endowed him with
a softer appearance than had the formal dark suit
she had seen him in before. But now, as they sat
at opposite ends of the sofa, Harriet was strongly
aware of just how superficial that impression was.

For somehow his shoulders seemed even broader
than at their first meeting, his legs longer and
harder, his wrists more sinuous, the lines of his face
more dramatically powerful.

To be frank, she was wishing he hadn't sat on
the sofa. His physical proximity disturbed her a
little.

She fought the feeling and narrowed her eyes at
him. 'Don't worry,' she told him. 'I'll have the
contents of this folder fixed in my mind, accurately

and in detail, long before we've touched down in Luxor.'

'There's a lot of information there. It will require a degree of mental effort.'

'Then I shall just have to apply the required degree of mental effort. Have no fear. I'm sure I can cope.'

'We shall see.'

Dexter Ross sat back in the leather sofa and reached for the whisky glass he had laid on the nearby coffee-table. Harriet watched as his long strong fingers closed round it. He had this ability to make every move he made watchable. He possessed a tensile, fluid grace that naturally drew the eye. As a dancer, Harriet found herself fascinated by this quality in him. But it was definitely the *only* thing about him she admired!

Not that he gives a jot for my admiration or the lack of it, she thought to herself wryly as he continued, 'I'm used to working with an assistant who knows her stuff. I don't have any patience with muddlers and amateurs.'

'Neither of which, presumably, you believe me to be...?' Harriet held the flint-sharp gaze a moment. 'Otherwise, it stands to reason, you would not have employed me.'

'As you say, it stands to reason.' He took a mouthful of his whisky. 'One does not knowingly recruit muddlers and amateurs.'

Neatly put. His statement left open the possibility that muddlers and amateurs might still slip through the net. Clearly, he had not ruled out that she might prove to be both.

Harriet regarded him across the sofa with a flicker of annoyance, irked at the way he so consistently misjudged her. He seemed so eager to believe the worst. Even his invitation to her to spend the night before their journey at his apartment had been accompanied by an observation that demonstrated little faith.

'It makes sense,' he'd told her. 'We can discuss last-minute details, and it'll avoid the hazard of your turning up late for the flight.'

What did he take her for? She'd snapped her response at him. 'I promise you I don't make a habit of missing planes!'

There had been no apology. 'And you won't miss this one, either,' he had responded calmly down the phone. 'I intend personally to see to it that you get there on time.'

Harriet narrowed her eyes at him now as she reached for her own drink. She could guess what lay behind this persistent lack of faith in her—he still entertained doubts about her state of mind. He still believed her to be incapacitated by a broken heart.

He was wrong, of course, she thought, stifling a painful flicker. In spite of her broken engagement, she was still functioning perfectly, and soon enough Dexter Ross would discover that for himself.

Still, the very fact, it had occurred to her, that he had gone ahead and hired her in spite of his evident reservations seemed to indicate that none of the other applicants for the job had come anywhere near passing the test. This assumption gave her a comforting sense of security. He might not like her—he had made no effort to hide that fact!—

but at least he had realised she was the best one for the job!

Sitting back in the sofa and swirling the ice-cubes in her martini, so that they tinkled pleasingly against the finely cut crystal, she observed, 'You mentioned another assistant. One, you say, who really knew her stuff.' She took a mouthful of her drink, observing as she did so that he had one other attribute—he mixed a mean martini! She watched him curiously. 'What happened to her?'

Dexter Ross shook his head. 'I'm afraid she fell by the wayside. Unfortunately, I was obliged to dispense with her services.'

'Fell by the wayside?' Harriet was aware of a cold shiver. There was something a little menacing about that callous explanation. 'Why did you have to dispense with her services?'

'She wasn't up to it. She fell ill. I had to bring her back to England.' He smiled without compassion. 'She was of no use to me whatsoever.'

'Poor girl.' Again, he had succeeded in shocking her, just as he had at their first meeting when he had revealed his selfish attitude to his collection of treasures. Only this time Harriet's sense of shock was doubled. This time he was referring not to some mere inanimate objects but to a living, suffering human being.

She asked with a touch of outrage, 'And what happened to her? Did she recover?'

'I expect so. She didn't come down with anything fatal.' He smiled, the dark eyes glinting with amusement at her outrage. 'I'm certainly hoping for a full recovery...' With a lift of his eyebrows he paused just long enough to allow Harriet to wonder if this, after all, was a belated expression of human feeling. But then he added, disabusing her of any such foolish notion, 'I'm going to need her again later in the year.'

'Then it stands to reason you're hoping she'll recover.' There was an undisguised bite of disapproval in her tone. 'It would be most inconvenient for you if she didn't.'

'Most.' He was shameless. He even smiled as he said it. He took another uncaring mouthful of his drink. 'As I said, when she's fit she's an excellent assistant. She and I have worked together for many years.'

That confession only made his blatant callousness worse—and caused Harriet to ask herself an uncomfortable question. How will he treat me, a virtual stranger, she wondered, if I should inflict on him the inconvenience of coming down with something? He'd taken the trouble, if without sympathy, to bring the other girl home. Me, she decided half seriously, he'd probably just kick under a sand-dune!

'So, what did she come down with?' Harriet watched him with narrowed gaze. 'It must have been quite serious if you had to fly her back to England.'

'A mixture of things. Gippy tummy. Heat exhaustion. She was quite incapable of work. There was no point in her staying on.'

As he smiled again and took another mouthful from his glass, those disconcerting black eyes of his never leaving her face, Harriet wondered if he was deliberately seeking to shock her. She suspected he probably was. He had no conscience. It amused him to flaunt his cold, uncaring heart.

'I'm surprised.' She swirled her ice-cubes and looked into the black eyes, hating the way they seemed to pierce through her. He can see everything I'm thinking, she thought with some resentment. He probably knows precisely what I'm about to say next!

She went ahead and said it anyway. 'I'm surprised to hear that. You said she'd been working with you for a number of years. I would have thought that by now she'd have become acclimatised to Egypt.'

Dexter shook his head. 'She was far from acclimatised. In the past we've always gone in winter. This was the first year she's ever had to cope with summer heat.'

Harriet didn't understand. 'You mean you only work in winter? I thought this Egyptology stuff of yours was an all-the-year-round job.'

'No, this Egyptology stuff of mine is strictly winter fare.' He repeated her faintly demeaning phrase with a twinkle that assured her that he was not even slightly demeaned. 'I normally go in December or January. These are the coolest months of the year.'

'I see.' She didn't really, but things were starting to fall into place a bit. 'So, does this mean you're only a part-time archaeologist? That all this...Egyptology stuff...' This time no insult was intended. She simply couldn't think of another phrase! 'Does this mean that it's really just a hobby?'

'If you want to call it a hobby...' He shrugged. 'I suppose it is. It's certainly not a full-time occupation. As you yourself pointed out the other day, digging around among ancient Egyptian ruins is unlikely to pay for office space in Mayfair.'

Or for the extensive residential accommodation in which they were currently sitting. Harriet regarded him frankly. 'So, what *does* pay for it?' she asked.

'My more orthodox, regular full-time employment.'

'Which is?'

Dexter smiled. 'My, aren't you curious?'

'It's a legitimate curiosity. I'd like to know who I'm working for.'

'And why do you need to know who you're working for? All you need to know is that I'm solvent and in a position to pay your wages.'

And he was certainly that, many times over! Solvency, quite patently, was not one of Dexter Ross's problems.

Still, Harriet was curious. She confronted his reticence. 'I can't see why you wouldn't want to tell me—unless, of course, you have something to hide.'

'You mean you think I might be a tomb robber, after all?' He smiled, amused, as he drained his glass and laid it down.

'Who knows? Perhaps you are. Or some modern-day equivalent.'

One dark eyebrow lifted. He was surprised by her boldness. To be honest, she was a little surprised by it herself.

'And if you discovered that I was,' he put to her, watching her, as, suddenly awkward, she dropped her eyes away from his, 'would you feel obliged to refuse to work for me? Would your scruples demand that you turn down the job?'

Harriet bit her lip. She wished she hadn't got into this. Scruples were definitely something she suffered from and she would indeed have to reconsider working for him if she found out he was a crook!

He was waiting for her answer. 'Well, would you?' he insisted.

Harriet hesitated, then breathed deeply. 'I might,' she confessed.

'Might you, indeed? That's very interesting.' He leaned back more comfortably, stretching his long legs—which really were, Harriet observed, quite extraordinarily long. 'So, what would your definition of a modern-day tomb robber be?'

Harriet shifted her gaze from the long stretch of leg. 'I have no idea. It's not something I've ever thought about.'

'Think about it now. I think we ought to get this clear.' He paused and laid one arm along the back of the sofa, causing her to shrink back in her seat as her heart leapt strangely. This man was all restless, predatory limbs!

'After all,' he was continuing, 'it would be most inconvenient for both of us if we were to discover, once we'd already got to Egypt, that the way I earn my living was incompatible with your scruples. Far better to get the whole thing sorted out now.'

It was the angle at which his head was tilted, causing the light from the table lamp to fall across his face, that suddenly caused Harriet, for the very first time, to notice the extraordinary quality of his lashes. They were so thick, so dark that they seemed drawn on with a pencil. How absolutely astonishing, she found herself thinking. I'd give my arm for lashes like that.

She tore her gaze away. Was she crazy? How could she pause to admire the wretched man's lashes when the one and only thing she desired at this moment was that he remove his arm from the back of the sofa—and preferably his entire person from the seat at the same time?

But he did not move a muscle. His eyes were on her. And it struck Harriet as she glanced up at him that he was waiting for something. Her heart fluttered as he confirmed this by demanding, 'Well?'

'Well, what?'

One eyebrow lifted. 'What do you have to say?'

Harriet swallowed drily, feeling an absolute idiot. It would appear that, while she'd been distracted, he'd asked her a question, and now he was expecting some kind of answer. She stared at him mutely. Her mind had gone blank.

It was that arm of his, she told herself crossly, that he had draped so casually along the sofa back, its sun-tanned extremity suddenly so close that she was afraid at any minute it might brush against her shoulder. He had no business sitting with his hand so close.

But he was still waiting. She cleared her throat and fought through her confusion. 'What do I have to say about what?' she croaked.

'I said, how does commodities brokering fit into your scheme of things? Is that a professional area your sensitive scruples can live with?'

Harriet had only a vague notion as to what commodities brokering was—something to do with buying and selling commodities like gold and zinc and steel, she guessed. But she nodded anyway and asked no questions.

He caught her eye. 'So, I just scrape by, do I?'

Harriet nodded again. 'It sounds quite acceptable.'

'Good. In that case, you'll be staying on, I take it? I suggest we mark the occasion with a final drink before bed.'

As he rose to his feet, sliding his arm away as he did so, it struck Harriet that her imagination had been playing tricks on her. Considering the length of the sofa—which she figured to be at least eight feet—there was no way his hand could have been anywhere near her shoulder. And yet she had been totally convinced that it was. She'd been as conscious of its nearness as though it were brushing against her.

She found that thought troubling without quite knowing why. It suggested an unbalanced degree of sensitivity with regard to a man to whom, common sense warned her, the only wise response was complete indifference and a total absence of any sensitivity whatsoever.

Harriet stared at his back as he picked up both their glasses and crossed the room to the bar in one corner. Indifference and insensitivity to a man like Dexter Ross were surely states of mind that would be easily nurtured. It would take only the minimum of exposure to him, she felt certain, for them to develop entirely spontaneously and naturally. That comforting thought made her feel much better.

She watched him as he mixed her another martini and poured a shot of whisky into his own glass, and again she was struck by the elegant power of his movements. He would make a good dancer, she thought to herself, smiling, wondering how he would take to that idea. He had the physical qualities she looked for in her pupils.

He turned then and approached her and took her by surprise. 'So, how's the broken heart? Are you learning to live with it?' He paused before the sofa and held out her drink to her. 'I hope at least you've got your grief under control. As I told you, I have no use for an assistant who spends her time pining after her lost lover while she's supposed to be working for me.'

It was the sheer unexpectedness of the remark that caused Harriet to flush and glance away quickly. Its callousness, too, had caused her heart to shift inside her. Just for an instant she could think of nothing to say.

He was still holding out her glass to her, standing over her, watching her with those eyes as hard as hatchet blades. A sudden smile touched his lips. 'But don't think me unmerciful. You're free to pine all you like when you're off duty, in your own time.'

'I won't be doing any pining.' But her eyes betrayed her, and her hand was unsteady as she reached out to take the glass. She had thought little of Tom over the past few days, since her luck had changed and her financial dilemma had been solved, and she certainly hadn't been doing any pining. But the wound he had inflicted had not yet quite healed, and Dexter's cruel words had scraped against it like a claw.

She took a mouthful of her drink to steady her shaken nerves. 'You really needn't worry yourself about my emotional state. It won't interfere with my work. I guarantee it.'

'I sincerely hope not.' As he spoke, he reseated himself at the other end of the long leather sofa. 'Otherwise our partnership will have a short and unhappy life. At the first sign of mooning you'll be on the first plane back to England.'

'There won't be any mooning.'

Harriet looked into his face, feeling chilled by that threat of instant dismissal and wondering just how serious he was. She didn't doubt his ruthlessness, but hadn't she already decided that the reason he had chosen her out of all the others was because she was the only one equipped to do the job? He was bluffing, she felt certain. He couldn't afford to lose her. All he was doing was trying to scare her.

Comforted by this thought, she went on to assure him with what, after all, was the absolute truth. 'I'm not an immature child, Mr Ross. I keep my professional life and my personal life strictly separate. I don't allow one to interfere with the other.'

One black eyebrow lifted. 'A most commendable philosophy. Indeed, one that I myself have long adhered to.' Then a flash of cynicism touched the dark eyes. His lips curled sceptically at the corners. 'Alas, however, in my experience it is a philosophy rarely to be found in women. If you are speaking the truth, you are indeed unusual.'

'And what is that supposed to mean?'

'It means quite simply that as a general rule women tend to be more emotional than men. And not only more emotional, less in control of their emotions.'

Harriet tilted her chin at him and laughed a scornful laugh. 'How exceedingly weak and messy of them!' she exclaimed. Then she added, 'Maybe it's because I grew up in an all-female house- hold——' for the most part there'd been just her mother, her younger sister and herself '—but I happen to believe that women's superior ability over men to keep in touch with their emotions is a strength, and not the weakness that men like you like to portray it as!'

'Men like me? And what type of man is that?'

That was a pretty colossal question! Harriet pulled a face and said nothing. Her answer was burning a hole in her tongue. But she ought to be discreet. After all, he was her employer!

'Go on. You can tell me.'

'I'd really rather not.'

'Are you afraid you might offend me?'

She would love to offend him, but she had no desire to lose her job! Her opinion of Dexter Ross was that he was arrogant and cold-hearted and in- capable of caring for anyone but himself. She smiled a careful smile. 'I think we ought to change the subject.'

'Why, are you afraid I might get angry? I thought you were the one who wasn't afraid of emotions?'

'I'm not afraid of emotions . . .' She would rather have kept silent, but the dark eyes were challenging her and she felt herself rising to the challenge. She looked straight at him. 'But I think you are.'

'Afraid? In what way?'

'Well, perhaps not afraid.' Fear, she sensed, would be as alien to him as compassion. 'But you don't like them. I suspect you find them inconvenient.'

'Sometimes they are. Most inconvenient.' Unabashed, he nodded in agreement. Then he threw her a look that reached to the core of her. 'Surely you know all about the inconvenience of emotions?'

It was a veiled, callous reference to her supposedly broken heart. Harriet felt herself draw back as though he had hit her. But then, as he continued to sit there and watch her with that superior, sadistic smile on his lips, she felt an angry, irrepressible urge to strike back.

She said, as though he had not spoken, 'That must make your personal life a little difficult.'

'In what sense difficult?'

'Perhaps I've chosen the wrong word. Perhaps barren is really the word I'm looking for.'

He took a mouthful of his drink, eyeing her as he did so. He's enjoying this, Harriet thought. He's wondering how far I'll go.

She was wondering the same as he proceeded to ask her, 'And why should you suppose that my personal life is barren?'

'How could it be otherwise when you have such an aversion to emotion? Personal relationships of any depth necessarily involve emotion.'

'Perhaps depth is not something I look for in my relationships. Perhaps I look for other things.'

'Like what, for example?'

'Like enjoyment. Like fun. Like two people simply having a good time together.'

His fingers seemed to caress the crystal whisky glass as he spoke. And, in spite of herself, as her eyes followed the movement, the sensuality in those long fingers sent a shiver down Harriet's spine.

And in the same instant she understood something.

Harriet had sensed as soon as she had walked into the penthouse that there was no long-term woman in Dexter Ross's life. The décor was wholly masculine, all leather and chrome and crystal. No female hand had left its imprint.

Yet there was something in the atmosphere that was unmistakably feminine. An aura. Yet more sensual. Almost like a perfume that seemed to hang like sweet incense in the air. It was the perfume, she realised now, of all the no-doubt countless women who had passed briefly through his penthouse and his life, selflessly dispensing fun and good times.

She wondered a little sadly if they had known that was their fate. To be used for a while and then discarded. Her heart caught inside her. She knew how that felt.

'You should try it some time.' He spoke suddenly, jolting her.

'Try what?' She blinked at him, not understanding.

'Try looking for a little less depth of emotion. Settle for something less demanding. Enjoy yourself.'

Harriet drained her glass right down to the ice-cubes. 'Depth of emotion and enjoyment are not,' she told him curtly, 'as you seem to believe, mutually exclusive.'

'I would say they are in your case.' He eyed her critically. 'Your last little liaison, if I may say so, didn't exactly leave you with a smile on your face.'

There was no denying that, so Harriet did not try to. She stared for a moment at the melting ice-cubes in her glass. Then she looked up into his face. 'No, but it left me wiser.'

'Let's hope so.' He drained his glass and laid it on the coffee-table. 'Let's hope it left you with at least enough wisdom not to screw up our forth-coming expedition. If you were to do that, you wouldn't emerge from that smiling, either.'

More threats. Harriet looked at him as he rose to his feet, announcing, 'It's getting late. I think I'll turn in now.' With every breath he took he grew more abominable, but she would not allow him to get under her skin. He had hired her, though he disliked her, because no one else could do the job, and though she disliked him equally she would stick the job out. She smiled to herself. Theirs was a pact drawn out of need. Neither one could do without the other.

It was a reassuring thought. In the skirmishes ahead—for there were bound to be skirmishes, that was inevitable—at least they would confront one another as equals. She might dislike him, but she had no cause to fear him.

She reached for the folder that still lay on the sofa. 'I think I'll make a start on this tonight, before I go to sleep.'

Dexter was standing over her, arrogant dark eyes on her. 'That's the right attitude. I'm pleased to hear it.'

Harriet rose to her feet and looked straight back at him. 'It really was not my intention to please you.'

There was a pause as they stood there, facing one another, the tall dark-haired man and the slim copper-haired girl, the blue eyes and the black locked together like vices, an aura of shimmering antipathy surrounding them.

And for a moment Harriet wondered if she had gone too far. She felt acutely aware of his almost tangible physicality and of the radiance of power that hung about him. A ruthless power, faintly menacing. His anger, she sensed, would be a terrible thing.

But there was no anger in his face, that harsh-lined dark-eyed face with the astonishing black eyelashes that she could see now at close range were even more astonishing than she'd realised. All there was was that familiar, amused look of arrogance.

He said, looking down at her, making her heart spurt strangely, 'I think that pleasing one another is something, my dear Miss Kaye, that you and I are destined never to achieve. The very best we can hope for is that we can work together in harmony. And, personally speaking, that for me will suffice.'

'Likewise.' For some reason her voice was croaky in her throat. Her mouth had gone dry. Her heart was beating too fast.

She was glad when he stepped away with a nod of satisfaction, and then with a brief, 'Goodnight,' headed in swift strides for the door.

But then, in the open doorway, he paused. 'Oh, by the way... I know you've been wondering, so

I may as well tell you ... how I came to choose you for the job.'

As Harriet blinked, he continued, 'Your physical fitness was the main factor. Most of the other girls were hopelessly out of shape... Your physical fitness and the fact that you're obviously mentally bright...'

Harriet smiled an 'I-told-you-so' sort of smile. Hadn't she known all along she was the only one for the job?

But he proceeded now to knock the smile from her face. 'However, there was another girl who was equally suitable... I couldn't decide between you, so I decided to flip a coin and keep the loser on stand-by, just in case...'

As Harriet blanched, he added with relish, 'I thought you ought to know that, should you disappoint me or in any way fail to meet the demands of the job, all I have to do to get myself a replacement is pick up the phone and call the other girl. She already has her visa. She's ready to step on the first plane.'

He held her eyes a moment, enjoying the way her gaze had faltered. Then with an arrogant smile he turned and left the room.

Harriet watched him go, her stomach turned to lead. So much for her illusions of indispensability! Suddenly her grasp on this job that meant so much to her felt quite terrifyingly flimsy.

CHAPTER THREE

EGYPT. Suddenly, there it was, spread out below
them, shimmering magically in the early evening
sunshine, as the plane circled down over Luxor to
land.

Harriet felt her heart lurch excitedly inside her
as she craned against the window to gaze down at
the scene. The stretch of the desert, endlessly
golden, the clutter of buildings bleached by the sun,
the occasional vivid green of a clump of palm-trees
and, flowing through it all, a ribbon of sparkling
blue, the mysterious, legendary, life-giving Nile.

'So, how does it look?' Dexter spoke suddenly,
leaning across her to look down at the view.

Harriet felt him brush her arm. Heat touched her
skin. It was an effort not to be silly and snatch her
arm away.

She answered, 'It looks breathtaking. Even more
breathtaking than I'd imagined.'

'It is rather breathtaking. I have to agree.' Dexter
glanced at her as he sat back in his seat once again,
and there was an expression on his face that quite
transformed him. A look of simple pleasure, with
no sign of his usual hardness.

He's pleased to be here, Harriet thought, thrown
a little. It was the first time she had seen him
looking pleased about anything!

Then his expression altered subtly. He glanced at
her mischievously. 'Wait till you step off the plane,'

he told her. 'That's when you'll realise how truly breathtaking it is.'

Harriet knew what he was meaning. 'Be prepared,' he'd warned her earlier, 'for heat like you've never known before.' When she stepped out of the plane she would have her first real test of coping with the heat that had defeated her predecessor, and she had a strong suspicion he'd quite enjoy seeing her fail it.

She turned back to the window. 'I can't wait to get off the plane. I can't wait to get out there and see what it's really like.'

If he was expecting her to dissolve in a sweaty puddle on the tarmac, she had every intention of disappointing him. If it killed her, she would remain cool and calm—and upright! She had to, or he would simply bundle her back on the plane, then pick up the phone and call her replacement!

And besides, it was true. She couldn't wait to get out there. Suddenly, she was filled with the excitement of Egypt. She longed to explore and discover this ancient land.

For the past five and a half hours, during their flight from London, Harriet had been poring over the contents of the folder. At first it had felt simply like a chore to be got through as she struggled with unfamiliar facts and names. But with every page she'd consumed she'd found her fascination growing for this country with its ancient, splendid history. She'd found herself absorbed in the contents of the pages, as she learned all about the long-ago pharaohs, the temples they had built themselves, and their fabulous tombs. What had started as a chore had rapidly become a pleasure.

Her total absorption in the contents of the folder had provided a second, most welcome function. It had meant that, for the greater part of the journey, between Dexter and herself there had been only the minimum of communication.

This had proved a great relief, for she'd rather been dreading the thought of their being stuck next to one another for hours on end—a prospect which, undoubtedly, had not appealed to him either. As he had so succinctly spelled out to her the previous evening, neither of them took pleasure in the company of the other!

But now, as the plane came down to land at Luxor, such thoughts were far from Harriet's mind. She was totally caught up in the excitement of the moment.

'You look like a child at Christmas.'

Dexter interrupted her reverie. And as she turned to look at him, Harriet could see amusement in his eyes. Was he mocking her and the grin she knew was spread across her face? Did he find her excitement naïve and childish?

She looked back at him squarely. 'I feel like a child at Christmas. And it's a wonderful feeling. Don't you ever feel like that?'

It was silly and illogical, but in asking the question she'd entertained the possibility that he might actually say yes. But he shook his head. 'No, I guess I don't.' The dark eyes smiled mockingly. 'But, as we've already discussed, I'm not equipped for such emotional responses. I lack your finely tuned female sensitivities.'

Harriet stared into his face and decided she had imagined—or misinterpreted—the look of simple pleasure she'd thought she'd seen there a moment ago. Probably it had been nothing more than a muscular twitch, or else he'd been thinking about something else entirely, something far more materialistic and worldly. It could not be down to the simple pleasure of arriving in Egypt. He was incapable of being moved by anything so trite.

Well, that's your loss, she was thinking, as she looked at him now. Her generous, loving nature exposed her to pain and treachery, but it also enabled her to drink the pleasures of life to the full.

She said, 'In that case, I can't help feeling sorry for you.'

But even as she said it, she knew it wasn't true. Pity was not an emotion that Dexter Ross aroused. Dislike. Distaste. Disapproval. All of these came naturally and easily. But the emotional hardness, the lack of caring in his character, though it might have in another, in him did not provoke pity.

His poise and self-possession placed him beyond the scope of pity. With admiration, not pity, was how most people would respond to him.

Perhaps he knew what she was thinking. He smiled that dark smile of his. 'Save your pity,' he told her, 'for those who need it.'

On that acerbic note the plane touched down in Luxor. Then, along with the handful of other first-class passengers, Harriet and Dexter were making their way to the exit and the steps that would lead them down to the little bus that was waiting to take them to the tiny airport terminal.

And as Harriet stepped out through the cabin door she paused and had to stifle a gasp of amazement. Dexter hadn't been kidding. The heat was like an oven!

The next half-hour or so passed in noisy, good-natured chaos as they made their way through Immigration, picked up their baggage and went outside to hire a cab. Then followed a feast of visual excitement as they made the fifteen-minute drive to their Nileside hotel.

Men in colourful galabiyahs, the traditional long robes of the country, rode along unhurriedly on donkeys. Groups of bright-eyed children smiled and waved at them. And everywhere were the coloured *calèches*, the horse-drawn carriages, favoured by tourists, with their bright decorations and polished brasses.

I'm going to enjoy this place, Harriet found herself thinking, momentarily forgetting her companion. There was something about it. Something in the air. Something, in spite of its strangeness, that drew her.

The hotel, as she had expected, was sumptuous and classy, their rooms the ultimate in luxury. Dexter had booked a suite that consisted of two separate bedrooms linked by a spacious, well-furnished sitting-room.

'We can use the sitting-room as our office,' he told her once the porter who had carried up their bags had departed and Dexter had phoned down to room service for some drinks. Then he smiled that mocking, arrogant smile of his. 'I can't see us wanting to use it for anything other than business. I doubt either of us will be anxious to spend our free time together.'

'No, I think that's most unlikely.' Harriet did not look at him. Instead, she crossed to the balcony windows, slid them open, and stepped outside to admire the magnificent view of the Nile. 'It would be a shame,' she added, aware that he had followed her, 'for us to spoil whatever free time we have by spending it together.'

'I couldn't agree more.' He was standing behind her. 'Considering how little free time we'll have, it would be an unforgivable shame.'

Harriet still did not look at him, but, as she stepped to the edge of the balcony, she had to stifle a flicker of perverse annoyance at the way her gibes so consistently failed to bother him. *Though I should be grateful,* she reproved herself. *If they bothered him, he might fire me, and that's the last thing I can afford to happen!*

She leaned against the balcony, feeling the hot sun on her skin, raising her face to it, basking in its warmth. And she wondered for a moment what it was about Dexter Ross that provoked those frequent gibes of hers. Ordinarily, it was not in her nature to be so verbally aggressive. *He simply brings out the worst in me,* she decided.

'That's where we'll be working.' Dexter had come to stand beside her. As she glanced round, he was pointing across the river.

'Is that the West Bank?' Harriet's eyes widened with interest. 'Is that where the Valley of the Kings is?'

'You can't see it from here. It's right out in the desert. But, yes, out there is the Valley of the Kings.'

'And the tomb of Horthot, where we'll be working?' Harriet beamed with excitement as he nodded. The notes in the folder were suddenly coming to life. 'How marvellous!' she exclaimed. 'I'm dying to see it.'

'You'll see it soon enough. Tomorrow at the crack of dawn, to be precise.'

He had said it to burst her bubble. Harriet knew that. To remind her she was here for work, not pleasure. But she remained defiantly buoyant as she turned to toss a glance at him.

'Marvellous,' she said again. 'I can't wait to get started.' Then she asked him a question that had occurred to her on the plane. 'Will we be going to the Valley of the Queens as well—or will you be concentrating solely on the tomb of King Horthot?'

'It depends how we progress. If we have enough time, we might make a sortie to the Valley of the Queens. Why? What particularly interests you there?'

'I thought it might be interesting to see the tomb of Horthot's wife. You mention her briefly in your notes.'

'Only very briefly.' His tone was dismissive. 'She's of no great interest. She wasn't important.'

'I don't suppose she was.' His dismissiveness annoyed her. She found herself adding with a little more emotion than was strictly necessary, 'At any rate, she wasn't important to her husband. After all, he abandoned her for another woman.'

Dexter turned round then to look at her. 'Does that fact upset you?'

'Upset me, no. I just think it's a little sad. She appears to have been a good woman, worthy of better treatment.'

Dexter smiled cynically. 'But then men, throughout history, are renowned for treating good women unfairly.' He paused and allowed his eyes to pierce right through her. 'It occurs to me that you have something in common with Horthot's wife. You appear to identify with her rather strongly. Perhaps a little more strongly than is wise.'

It took Harriet a moment to understand what he was getting at. She frowned. 'I don't know what you mean.'

'I think you do.' His eyes burned like hot cinders. 'I think you know very well what I mean.' His lips thinned with impatience. 'Remember my warning. At the first sign of mooning you're on the next plane home.'

So, that's what he was getting at! Harriet blanched. 'But that's ridiculous! You think I was thinking about my fiancé? Well, I wasn't. I was——'

'Frankly, I'm not interested in the details. Frankly, I'm not interested in anything about it. And I would advise you, if you want to keep your job, to drop the subject now.'

'But—'

He was so wrong! She hadn't been thinking of Tom, and she definitely had not identified with Horthot's wife! If she'd been thinking of anyone, she'd been thinking of Dexter! For it had struck her that he had more than a bit of the pharaoh in him, not least in the cavalier way he treated his women.

But, before she could say more, she was interrupted by a sudden tapping on the inner sitting-room door.

'That must be room service with our drinks.' With a final sharp glance at her, Dexter turned away. 'You stay where you are. I'll get it.'

As he disappeared indoors, Harriet turned to face the river, with its barges and graceful *feluccas* gliding by. He had accused her wrongly. She had not been mooning. In fact, if the truth were told, not once since they'd left London had she even given Tom a thought.

What was more, she realised, when Dexter had sprung the subject on her a moment ago, she hadn't felt the slightest bit upset. She congratulated herself silently. That was a definite improvement.

She was still watching the river when Dexter reappeared, striding through the balcony doorway with a waiter at his heels. Harriet turned to watch him as he instructed the waiter, 'Bring the tray out here, please. We'll have our drinks out on the balcony.' He paused and cast a quick glance in Harriet's direction. 'Unless, of course, you find it too hot out here?'

Harriet might have opted for the air-conditioned sitting-room had it not been for that confrontational glint in his eye. What he was really asking her was, Can you stand it, or are you too going to be a casualty of the fierce Egyptian heat?

As the waiter hovered by the table that stood in the middle of the balcony, waiting for her confirmation of Dexter's instructions, she crossed with a flourish to smilingly seat herself on one of the chairs that surrounded the table.

'Oh, no,' she insisted. 'I wouldn't dream of going indoors. I'd much rather sit out here in the sun.'

Quite unjustly a moment ago he had accused her of mooning. She was not about to provide him with another opportunity for criticism!

The waiter took his cue and laid the tray down on the table, then departed, leaving the two of them alone. Dexter sat down opposite Harriet and pushed her orange juice towards her.

'This should help you recover,' he said.

'Recover from what?'

It was a valid enough question, but she said it too quickly and it sounded defensive. Inwardly, she groaned, knowing what he would suspect.

'The journey. The heat. The early start.' He took a mouthful of his beer, his eyes never leaving her. Then in an ironical tone he added the opposite of what he was clearly thinking. 'Surely, you have nothing else to recover from?'

'Absolutely. Nothing.'

'Good. I'm glad to hear it.' He laid his beer glass on the table, closing the subject.

Harriet looked back at him. It was ridiculous, she was thinking. With anyone else she would have simply said straight out that he was wrong to believe she was mooning after Tom. But there was something about that cutlass-sharp gaze of his that disoriented her and caused her to lose the power of rational argument. She just knew that as soon as she tried to defend herself she would simply end up wading even deeper into trouble.

Why he should have this effect on her she had no idea. All she knew was that, increasingly, it was so—and that in the circumstances the wisest thing she could do was keep her mouth shut on the subject of her personal life.

He was leaning back in his seat, his eyes fixed beyond the balcony on some spot off towards the horizon. Harriet picked up her orange juice and let her gaze follow his. 'Tell me about the work we're going to be doing,' she asked him.

'I thought you'd read the notes?' He did not turn to look at her. 'If you've read and understood them, you ought to know already what we'll be doing.'

'I've read the notes, and I've understood them, but mostly what I've learned is what you've been doing in the past.' In spite of the hostility in his response, Harriet felt herself relax a little. At least on matters relating strictly to work she could handle her responses to him without any difficulty. 'I'd like to know what we're going to be doing for the next four weeks.'

He did look at her then. 'Really just more of the same. The tomb of King Horthot that I started working on last year still has a lot of work to be done on it. That's what we'll be concentrating on for the most part.'

Harriet leaned towards him. 'You mean restoring the wall paintings? That's what your notes are mostly about.'

'The wall paintings. Precisely.' He leaned back in his chair, stretching his long legs out in front of him. 'The ones we've uncovered are in remarkably good condition, considering they're a couple of thousand years old. I'm hoping that with a bit of luck we might find some more.'

As he spoke, Harriet was aware of a subtle change in him. His expression had grown softer. His tone had grown warmer. She was reminded of that look of his she'd seen in the plane. Perhaps he *is* capable of caring about something, after all, she thought, even if it is just a bunch of ancient Egyptian tomb paintings!

She felt drawn by the change in him. She leaned towards him curiously. 'How did you get involved in all of this? It's not exactly a common hobby, Egyptology.'

'By chance, I suppose. The way these things happen. I was pretty young. Still no more than a child.'

'What drew you to it? What attracted you?' Suddenly, she was really interested to know.

He looked back at her, an amused but oddly veiled look in his eyes. 'Perhaps it was my materialistic, acquisitive instincts that drew me into Egyptology. Perhaps all I was looking for was some excuse to go raiding ancient tombs and stealing treasures for myself.'

Harriet met the veiled dark gaze. She knew he was joking. But though she responded with a smile, she knew it was possible that what he said was actually the truth. As she had already decided, this man was capable of anything.

She put to him, playing along with his humour, 'So, why didn't you become a full-time archaeologist? Then you'd have had even more opportunities to acquire treasures for your collection.'

'I thought about it.' His eyes swept over her, seeming to read every shadow and nuance of her expression.

He knows what I think of him and it merely amuses him, Harriet realised with an expected flash of admiration. How could one fail to admire such total self-possession?

'But I decided,' he was continuing, 'that it was probably better to do it on a part-time basis. That way I'm able to finance myself. I don't have to rely on grants and commissions. I can initiate my own projects. I can choose what I want to work on.' He smiled. 'To indulge one's passions one must have funds.'

Harriet nodded. 'Yes.' But the word stuck in her throat. Without realising it, he had touched upon a sensitive spot. A source of funds, she thought bitterly. That was all I was to Tom.

She slid her eyes away, knowing how they might betray her, reached for her glass of orange juice and drained it. Then with a composed smile she rose to her feet and told him, 'If you don't mind, I think I'll go and unpack now.' She glanced at her watch. 'It'll soon be time for dinner. I'd like to have a shower and change.'

'Go ahead. I'm going to stay and watch the sunset.' His eyes were on her. 'You should watch it, too. Egyptian sunsets are quite spectacular. Excellent therapy for the soul.'

Harriet had been about to move off, but there was something in the way he'd said that that caused her to hesitate for just a moment. And it was in that moment, as she paused to frown down at him, that he reached out his hand and caught hold of her arm.

As she looked down at him, startled, the dark eyes burned into her. 'Let it go,' he rasped at her, his tone fierce and impatient. 'Stop punishing yourself. I can't believe he was worth it!'

Harriet could not speak. Her mouth had turned to cardboard. She stared at him mutely, her senses overcome by the look of fierce intensity that burned from his eyes and seemed to flood into her, like molten electricity, through the steely-hard fingers of the hand that held her arm.

'Take my advice. Watch the sunset. Take your mind off it! Do yourself some good!'

As he shook her impatiently, Harriet stared at him, bewildered. Bewildered at her own totally paralysed reaction to this outrageous and unexpected assault, and bewildered too by the expression on his face. For though there was impatience there, and anger, there was also a glimmer of something else.

But then whatever it was vanished. Almost roughly, he pushed her from him, releasing his grip on her as he did so. 'I hope you were listening. That was your last warning!' he grated.

Though she was free now, Harriet's legs still felt like jelly. She stood, gasping for breath, unable to move.

Then he turned away abruptly to stare out over the balcony. 'Go and do your unpacking and leave me to watch the sunset in peace.'

'That will be my pleasure.'

At last she found her voice. But Harriet's legs still felt as though they could barely support her as she turned and headed swiftly for the sanctuary of her own room.

It took Harriet a little while to recover her equilibrium.

Safely back in her room, she unpacked then took a shower and, wrapped in a big, soft towel, sat down thoughtfully on the bed.

That had been quite a little scene—and all over nothing! Dexter seemed to have the knack of picking up her tiniest reaction and then blowing it up out of all proportion! For he really was wrong about her feelings for her ex-fiancé!

She glanced at her reflection in the big wall mirror. He'd got off on the wrong tack with that business about Horthot's wife and his assumption that Harriet identified with the poor woman. And perhaps she had reason to, but she didn't.

Certainly there were similarities in their two stories—Harriet's and that of the two-thousand-year-old queen. Dexter was quite right in his assumption about that. For both Harriet and the ancient queen had been unceremoniously abandoned in favour of another woman. The queen's husband had gone off with a young serving girl, leaving her bereft and broken-hearted, while Tom, Harriet's fiancé, while on a two-month trip to America, had unexpectedly married someone else.

But the big difference was that Harriet was not broken-hearted.

She'd been shocked and stunned by Tom's betrayal, and by the way he hadn't even had the guts to tell her personally, but had left her to find out the truth from a friend. She'd felt pole-axed by the news. She'd been crushed and humiliated to learn how cynically Tom had used her. But her heart, it had to be said, had not been broken.

That was something she had suspected right from the start, though it was really only gradually, over the past few days, that she had become absolutely certain that it was the case. In spite of what had happened, her heart was intact.

With a wry smile Harriet shook back her copper-brown hair. That made it sound a little too easy, she reflected, as though she'd emerged unscathed from Tom's betrayal. And that was not the case, for he had wounded her deeply and the wound would take a while to heal. But luckily that wound had not been inflicted on her heart—for, though she had been fond of Tom, she had never been in love with him. The emotion that had drawn her to him most strongly was admiration.

She sighed now. What an error of judgement she'd made, mistaking what he did for what he was. As a man, she now knew, he was worthless, beneath contempt, and perhaps she might have realised that a great deal sooner had she not allowed herself to be blinded by admiration for his work. His work which, over their two years together, she herself had helped to fund.

Tom's field of work was cancer research and he was a brilliant and dedicated scientist. But he was also penniless, living on meagre grants. And Harriet knew for sure that if she hadn't been around to bale him out financially over the past couple of years he would not have been able to continue his vital work.

And Harriet believed in his work as fervently as he did. The money she had given to help him she had given gladly. And even now she did not regret it.

But what she did regret, and deeply, was the final, bitter chapter.

For she had learned more than the mere fact of his sudden marriage when she had gone in desperation to speak to his friend after weeks of unan-

swered letters and phone calls. She had learned also
about the callous way Tom had tricked her out of
the money she had saved for the building repairs.
And that she was not prepared to forgive.

He had told her the grant he needed to go to
America—on a long-planned trip to further his research—had been held up and that without it he
would have to cancel his trip.

'If you lend me the money, I'll wire it back to
you as soon as possible,' he'd promised her faith-
fully, knowing she would not fail him.

And so she'd written the cheque, crossing her
fingers that the grant would arrive before she
needed to pay the builders.

But the so-called loan, she had learned in the end,
was destined almost certainly never to be repaid.
For Harriet knew now that Tom had lied to her.

He had never needed her money. He had already
had the grant. As a final gesture before deserting
her for another woman, he had simply stolen from
her the cash he knew she needed so badly.

She frowned at her reflection. What an idiot she'd
been. She should have been able to see what kind
of man he was. A greedy, grasping taker. A man
with no personal scruples.

But a clever and convincing one, she reminded
herself in fairness. Hadn't he fooled her mother and
sister as well? They'd been almost as devastated as
she was by what had happened.

And here I am getting involved with another one
from the same mould! As she stood up from the
bed, she thought of Dexter Ross. He, too, was a
greedy, grasping taker. Only this time, thank
heavens, the involvement was purely professional.

Dexter Ross would never have the power to hurt her.

She crossed to the window and glanced out over the balcony. It was dark, the night sky studded with stars. It suddenly occurred to her that she had missed the sunset.

That thought caught her unawares. She felt a jolt inside her as suddenly she was thrown back to that moment on the balcony when Dexter had reached out and grabbed her by the arm. Once again she felt her flesh burn and her heart gallop in her chest. Once again she felt gripped by a sense of paralysis.

She thrust the feeling from her. She had reacted stupidly. It was the surprise that had done it. He had caught her unawares.

Harriet glanced at her watch. It was after eight o'clock. It was time she got dressed and went downstairs for dinner.

She shrugged off her towel and stepped towards the wardrobe. From now on, she was thinking, she would be on her toes. She would not allow him to surprise her again.

But Dexter had a talent for springing surprises, as Harriet was very soon to discover.

For half an hour later, as she stepped out of the lift into the lobby on her way to the dining-room, Harriet was presented with a spectacle that caused her to stop in her tracks, her eyes wide with astonishment, her jaw dropping open.

'Good grief!' she murmured. 'I don't believe it!'

CHAPTER FOUR

THEY were standing by the fountain in the middle of the lobby, blissfully unaware of Harriet's presence, smiling at one another and embracing—Dexter and a stunning dark-haired girl!

Well, how about that? Harriet thought as she watched them. He has a girlfriend here in Luxor!

Later, as she sat alone at her table in the dining-room, it occurred to Harriet that that wasn't so surprising. Hadn't she already decided that Dexter was a man with many women in his life?

What was surprising, however, she decided, as she poured herself another glass of wine, was the kind of girl his girlfriend was. That and the easy closeness she had witnessed between them. This was no fly-by-night romance.

At least not, Harriet felt certain, as far as the girlfriend was concerned. She was clearly a serious and respectable young woman, not the type to indulge in a frivolous romance—which was the only type of romance Harriet could imagine Dexter being involved in!

In her mind's eye she saw again that calm, beautiful face and the way it had lit up as Dexter had bent to kiss her. Did the girl know, Harriet wondered, what type of man she was dealing with? Was she aware that there were countless other women in his life?

No, of course she didn't. Why would she even suspect it when Dexter was such a clever actor? He, too, had appeared enthralled by their reunion in the lobby. He had taken hold of her and hugged her with such warmth and passion, as though she were more special to him than anything in the world.

But then men were good at that. Harriet thought of Tom. Hadn't he been unstinting in his declarations of affection and gratitude? 'How I love you,' he'd used to tell her, 'you wonderful girl!'

And then, just like that, he'd dropped her from his life and gone off and married another girl.

She narrowed her eyes. Yes, the more she thought of it, the more she realised Dexter was just like Tom. An unscrupulous taker, in every sense of the word. A man who took not only things material, but human affection, trust and loyalty, nurturing and encouraging the generosity of others, and giving nothing in return.

She drank back her wine, congratulating herself quietly on having so accurately and speedily summed him up. It was just a pity, she reflected, that with people like him there was little one could do to halt their selfish progress. They just went on taking, moving from victim to victim, never giving a thought to the damage they were doing.

She gazed into her wine glass as though into a crystal ball. If only I could find a way to thwart you, Dexter Ross, how much pleasure that would give me!

Little did she realise that a perfect opportunity was waiting just around the corner!

*   *   *

Next morning, after breakfast on the balcony of her room, Harriet dressed quickly in a pair of khaki cotton trousers, a simple white blouse and slip-on canvas shoes.

'Don't wear sandals,' Dexter had warned her. 'They'll just let in the sand and that'll irritate your feet.'

Then she was hurrying downstairs to meet Dexter in the lobby, at six-thirty precisely, as they had arranged.

Dexter emerged from the dining-room at the very instant she appeared, looking sharp and self-assured, just as he always did. Like a man, Harriet reflected with a flicker of irritation, who has, and who knows he has, the world on a leash.

His evening with his beautiful girlfriend clearly hadn't done him any harm!

'Good morning. I see you made it. Have you had breakfast?' He was dressed in sand-coloured trousers and shirt. In one hand he carried a plastic bag. Without waiting for Harriet's answer, he held it out to her. 'In here is our water supply for the day. Two large bottles of mineral water. In future, I'll expect you to organise that. Since this is your first day, I've done it for you.'

So he had started already, Harriet observed with a grimace. The day had barely begun and he was already into his pharaoh act, throwing his weight around and snapping his fingers.

She responded with a forced smile. 'How kind of you,' she answered.

He smiled right back at her with a smile as false as her own. 'Kindness was really not my intention.

I simply did it in order to save time. I want to get on the road and get started without delay.'

'Then let's get on the road. I'm ready if you are.' She looked him in the eye. Lord, he was abominable.

'Are you quite sure you're ready? That you've got everything you'll need? Your tape recorder, your torch? Spare tapes, spare batteries?'

Harriet patted her bag. 'Everything,' she assured him. 'I told you, I'm a very well-organised person. I promise you you don't have to keep checking up on me.'

'And you did have breakfast?'

'Yes. In my room.'

'I hope you had something fairly substantial. Lunch, I'm afraid, is a long way off.'

'Don't worry, I'll survive.'

'Let's hope so.' He smiled at her, a smile as caring and compassionate as a crocodile's. 'We wouldn't want your first day also to be your last.'

As he said it, he turned away, heading across the lobby to the automatic doors that led out into the hotel forecourt. But Harriet had caught the subtle warning in the remark. Her replacement was just a phone call away should she inconveniently happen to fall by the wayside!

She glared at his back as she followed him outside and found herself thinking with a flash of irony of that touching reunion she had witnessed last night. His side of it had been faked. She was absolutely sure of that. Dexter Ross was incapable of human emotion.

Outside, with a peremptory snap of his fingers, he summoned one of the taxis that were lined up, waiting for passengers. Then, after a lengthy discussion with the driver—in Arabic, Harriet noted, as she had noted also yesterday, thoroughly impressed, in spite of herself—he was pulling open the door to allow her to climb into the back seat before taking the front seat next to the driver.

Harriet sat back in her seat and peered excitedly through the window as, once out of the hotel grounds, they made their way quickly between the horse-drawn *calèches*, the bicycles and the donkeys to the Corniche, the road that ran along the side of the Nile.

It was just after six-thirty, but already the streets were busy. In Luxor the day obviously got off to an early start!

A few minutes later they had arrived at the little jetty where a ferry was waiting to take them across to the West Bank. And Harriet was aware, as they set off, that she was grinning from ear to ear with delight.

Like a child at Christmas, as Dexter had so disparagingly described her. She wondered, as she cast a quick glance in his direction, if he was secretly laughing at her now. Even if he was, she was far too excited to care.

Once they reached the West Bank Dexter hailed another taxi, and again, before they climbed inside, there followed a lengthy, even somewhat emotional, discussion with the driver. But even though, as before, the conversation was conducted in Arabic, Harriet suddenly sensed she knew what it was about.

She felt a surge of disapproval. What he'd been doing was haggling. Shamelessly beating down the

drivers' fares. How could he, she thought, a man
of his wealth, behave in so mercenary a fashion in
a poor country like this? Judging by the age of their
taxis and their clean but shabby dress, the taxi
drivers didn't have two spare pennies to rub
together!

But she already knew the answer to her question.
He could do it because he was a heartless, uncaring
swine.

The drive through the desert was a breathtaking
experience, along a ribbon of road cut between
rocky outcrops, the sand a dazzle of every shade
of gold beneath a sky of perfect, uninterrupted
blue.

Then, at last, they were entering the Valley of the
Kings, with its tombs cut out of the living rock face,
and the taxi was setting them down outside the tomb
of Horthot, before turning around and heading
back the way they'd come.

'That's the last we'll be seeing of him until
lunchtime,' Dexter told her. 'If you want to go back
before then, I'm afraid you're going to have to
walk.'

The remark was accompanied by the usual
mocking smile. Harriet met the dark gaze. 'And
why would I want to go back?'

Dexter shrugged. 'Who knows? Stranger things
have happened. It was more or less right on this
very spot that your predecessor collapsed.'

Harriet felt herself flinch as she glanced down at
the ground, imagining the poor girl lying there, with
Dexter standing furiously over her.

She glanced up into his face. 'How very thoughtless of her. That must have messed up your entire day.'

'It messed up several entire days. And it would be most inconvenient if it were to happen again.'

As he spoke, Harriet had suddenly become aware of the sun, beating down like a furnace against her back. It was still only just after seven, but already the temperature was soaring. He hadn't been joking about the heat.

But she straightened her spine and looked back at him unflinchingly. 'You needn't worry. It won't happen again. I wouldn't dream of inconveniencing you.'

Dexter held her eyes a moment, the black gaze boring into her. Then he observed, 'You really do need this job badly. You need the money a hell of a lot.' He smiled a satisfied smile. 'I find that reassuring. It means you'll put up with whatever I care to throw at you.'

'I wouldn't bank on that.' Harriet glared at him. 'No?'

'Definitely not. I need the job, but there are limits.'

He simply smiled. 'In that case it will be interesting to see just how far those limits can be stretched.'

Then, before she could answer, he was turning on his heel and leading her towards the entrance of the tomb, stepping past the guards who sat dozing in the doorway and into the dimly lit interior.

'Watch your step,' he was saying, as he led her towards a ramp that stretched between the entrance and the first chamber. 'Hang on to the handrail. It's rather a long drop.'

Harriet paused in her contemplation of his arrogance—no doubt he *would* enjoy stretching the limits of her patience!—and instead wisely concentrated on his warning and on the evidence of her own eyes as they grew accustomed to the dim light. For she could see that the narrow wooden ramp they were crossing was slung across what appeared to be a bottomless dark pit.

'In the old days there were no ramps. The idea was to deter tomb robbers,' Dexter was explaining, as she glanced down with a shudder. 'Little did they realise that the minute they stepped through the front door they would find themselves tumbling to their death.' He smiled an amused smile over his shoulder. 'An ancient but fairly effective method of burglar control.'

'Most effective.' Harriet shuddered again in agreement. And simultaneously it occurred to her that there were certain modern-day tomb robbers whom she would not be too sorry to see meet such a fate!

The one who particularly sprang to mind was glancing back at her over his shoulder, almost as though he could read her thoughts. 'But they were ingenious, these ancient tomb robbers. After a couple of fatalities, they learned their lesson and simply stopped using the front door. Instead, they burrowed in through the side walls—which is how most of the tombs came to be stripped of their treasures centuries before people like me came along.'

One could tell he felt an affinity with these ancient tomb robbers. He admired their ingenuity, their stealth, their cunning. The very same attributes, Harriet reflected with disapproval, that he no doubt had employed to amass his own collection of treasures!

Dexter proceeded to lead her through a labyrinth of chambers—some lit by fluorescent lamps fixed close to the ground, some unlit, which was why they needed their torches—to the tiny chamber where they would be working.

'It's still more or less as it was when it was found,' he told her. He gestured at the dust and debris everywhere. 'What I'm trying to do is find out just what we've got here.'

It was a painstaking job, Harriet soon discovered, as he got down to work on the chamber walls, cleaning away the accumulated dirt of centuries to uncover the magnificent paintings beneath.

Fascinated, Harriet watched him, trying to anticipate his needs, like a theatre nurse working with a surgeon, handing him the brushes and other implements as he needed them, and keeping the tape recorder constantly ready for when he wanted to dictate some notes.

She could scarcely believe that four hours had passed when he suddenly glanced at his watch and announced, 'I think it's time we took a short break. Let's go back to the mouth of the cave and have a breath of fresh air.'

A breath of fresh air was an optimistic description. They reached the mouth of the tomb to find the sun beating down and the air all around them almost too hot to breathe. But it was pleasant, all the same, to be out in the open again, Harriet reflected as she squatted down in the shade.

And suddenly she understood why he had asked her at the interview whether she suffered from claustrophobia. Anyone who suffered even mildly from that affliction wouldn't have lasted five minutes down in that dusty little chamber!

Dexter had seated himself at the opposite side of the cave mouth and was now rummaging in the bag where he kept the water bottles. First he handed her hers, then he surprised her as he produced from the bag's depths a packet of plastic-wrapped sandwiches. 'Just something to take the edge off your hunger,' he told her. 'Though in future, of course——'

'It'll be my job,' Harriet finished for him, 'to organise the sandwiches when I organise the water.'

'Ten out of ten.' As he met her eyes, he smiled. 'I'm glad you're proving to be such a willing little helper.'

Harriet grimaced. 'I'm glad you're glad,' she responded.

He ignored the undertow of sarcasm in her remark. 'Perhaps, after all, we'll work well together.' He held out one of the plastic-wrapped sandwiches. 'Just continue to do exactly as I tell you and we shouldn't have any problems.'

Harriet avoided his gaze and reached for her sandwich. How she loathed him when he started laying down the law!

'By the way, I ought to mention…' As her fingers closed round the sandwich, he did not release it. He held her eyes. 'You did a good job this morning. I was most impressed.'

Condescending swine! And yet, foolishly, she felt pleased. She had given him her best effort and recognition felt good.

Normally, she would have smiled and nodded her appreciation, but suddenly all she could think of, as he continued to hold on to the sandwich, was should she continue to hold on to it too or should she let it go?

I'm going crazy, she thought, unable to detach her gaze from his, oddly paralysed by the way their fingers were almost touching and by the dangerous dark look she could see flickering in his eyes.

She said, struggling for calm, still holding on to the sandwich, 'Don't sound so surprised. I told you I could do the job.'

'Yes, you did, and so far you've been proved right. Let's just hope you continue as you've started.'

'I'll do my best.'

'Good girl.' He held her eyes. Then, at last, he released his hold on the sandwich. 'Just keep your mind on the job and follow my orders.'

Harriet stared for a minute at the sandwich in her hand. It had survived the ordeal better than she had! For, shameful and ludicrous though it was, inside she was shaking. Her heart was pumping like a piston.

What the devil's got into me? she demanded impatiently, unwrapping the sandwich and taking a bite of it. Down in the narrow confines of the cave where they'd been working, strangely enough, she'd felt totally at ease with him. Now, out in the open, where she should feel less threatened, suddenly she found his proximity oppressive.

That's because out here there's just him and me,
she decided, watching as he proceeded to demolish
his own sandwich. Down in the cave their work
acted as a kind of buffer. But it still made no sense
that she suddenly felt so unhinged!

She glanced across at him with hostility. 'You
enjoy issuing orders.'

He looked back at her equably. 'Is that a
statement or a question?'

Harriet smiled a mocking smile. 'Definitely a
statement. No one in their right mind would consider it a question that needs asking.'

He nodded. 'If you say so.' He chewed for a
moment. Then he put to her, 'And you? Do you
enjoy taking orders?'

'Enjoy? No, I don't think I actually enjoy it ...
But I'm prepared to accept that I have no choice.
Within certain limits, as I mentioned before.'

'Yes, you did mention limits. And I seem to remember telling you that I'm going to rather enjoy
testing those limits of yours.'

He was laughing at her. Teasing her. Harriet was
aware of that. The look in the jet-black eyes was
light-hearted. And perhaps that was partly what ir-
ritated her so much—that he should remain so in
control when she felt so oddly vulnerable. For all
at once she did feel inexplicably vulnerable.

It was that silly game with the sandwich, she told
herself, and the *frisson* of danger she'd felt as she'd
looked into his eyes.

Defensively, in an effort to shake his poise a little,
she looked at him and said, 'I won't let you exploit
me. I'm not one of your poor, defenceless taxi
drivers.'

'Poor, defenceless taxi drivers?' He seemed genuinely puzzled. The straight black eyebrows drew together. 'I'm afraid you'll have to explain what you mean.'

Harriet instantly felt better. 'My pleasure,' she told him. If only fleetingly, she had him at a disadvantage. 'What I'm referring to,' she elaborated, 'is your behaviour this morning. The way you haggled with those two taxi drivers. That was exploitative and, in my view, shameful.'

To her annoyance, Dexter smiled. 'Shameful?' he echoed. 'Aren't you aware that haggling is a way of life in Egypt? Everybody does it all the time.'

'Yes, I know that.' She'd read that in her guidebook. 'But there's haggling and haggling. From the length of your discussions, I got the impression that you were beating them down rather a lot. And the second taxi driver,' she added sharply, 'actually seemed to be rather upset.'

He took a moment to respond, but he did not deny any of it. He simply said, 'The Egyptians are a very emotional people.'

'I see! That's why you treat them so badly. We both know how you despise people who can't control their emotions!'

The anger she felt was cleansing. As it went rushing through her, her earlier sense of vulnerability instantly dispersed.

She threw him a hard look. 'Aren't you ashamed of yourself?'

'And why should I be ashamed?'

'Because you're rich and they're poor. Because, unlike them, you don't need the money. A couple of pounds doesn't matter to you, but to these two taxi drivers it matters a great deal. It probably takes them months to earn what you earn in a minute.'

'Yes, you're right, it probably does.'

'And you still don't feel ashamed?' His attitude was shocking, though what else had she expected? 'Don't you feel bad about exploiting these poor people like that?'

'I have no problem whatsoever with the way I behaved.' He had leaned back a little so his eyes were in shadow, as though there were something he wished to hide from her. His rotten, guilty heart, Harriet decided, watching him. Yes, she'd been right. He was exactly like Tom.

Then he spoke again. 'Forgive me,' he told her, 'if I find your pronouncements on matters financial not altogether worthy of being taken seriously. If you don't mind, I prefer not to heed the advice of someone who is incapable of running her own small business with sufficient efficiency to ensure she can pay her bills.'

She had not expected that. Harriet flushed crimson. 'You're wrong. I pay my bills,' she answered tightly.

'Oh, sure, when someone comes along to rescue you.' His tone was dismissive. 'You may be a competent dancer, but, as a businesswoman, it's clear you're pretty useless.'

'No, I'm not! That's not fair! You don't know anything about my financial affairs!'

'I know they're in a mess, or else you wouldn't be here with me. So, what other deduction can I make other than that you're a totally useless businesswoman?'

'I'm a damned good businesswoman!' Harriet was choking with indignation. 'It wasn't my fault that I lost that money! I had it, but he took it from me! I trusted him and he cheated me! If it wasn't for him, I wouldn't need to be here!'

She bit her lip. She had not meant to say so much. But it had all come pouring out in an unstoppable torrent. She dropped her gaze to her lap, aware that she was trembling and that there were tears of emotion standing in her eyes.

A long silence followed. She could feel Dexter's eyes on her, cutting into her like lances. Her little outburst, she sensed, had been a terrible mistake.

Then he began to stand up. 'If you've finished eating,' he told her, 'I suggest we get back to work without delay.' His tone was controlled, but she could tell that he was angry.

No wonder, she acknowledged, as, not daring to speak, she followed him back across the ramp and through the maze of little chambers that led to the room where they were working. He had warned her against mooning, and what had she done instead? She had subjected him, this man with his aversion to messy emotions, to what he would interpret as an unforgivable display of the sufferings of her bleeding, broken heart.

But that was not what it had been. What had provoked her reaction was a sense of indignation at the total unfairness of his judgement. Though why that should matter to her she could not begin to imagine.

It was because she was so preoccupied with these thoughts that she failed to notice, until they were back in the chamber, that she had left her bag behind.

'Oh, blast!' As he turned to look at her, Harriet frowned in annoyance. 'I've forgotten my bag. I'll have to go back for it. I must have left it where we were sitting.'

His expression, already dark, now grew as black as thunder. 'So, this is the start. I was right, after all.'

'No, you weren't. It's nothing.' Harriet knew what he was saying. He was saying that, after all, she was unfit for the job. As panic seized her, she tried to force a smile. 'A moment of inattention; that's all it was. And it'll only take me a couple of minutes to go back and fetch it.'

'A couple of minutes we can ill afford to waste.' His tone was unforgiving. Her smile had not moved him. Then he added, 'I suppose I ought to go back with you.'

'There's no need. I can find my way on my own. We needn't both waste time.'

'If you're sure you can manage...?'

'Absolutely sure.' Decisively, Harriet turned away. 'You can start without me. I'll be as quick as I can.'

In fact, she made it back to the mouth of the cave in double-quick time. And there, to her great relief, precisely where she'd left it, on a jutting shelf of rock, lay her shoulder-bag.

She swung it over her shoulder with a sigh of satisfaction, then turned round and headed back across the ramp, shining her torch into the semi-gloom before her. At this rate she would be back before Dexter had time to miss her!

But it was just a couple of minutes later, as she was making her way across one of the chambers, that Harriet was struck by a sense of unfamiliarity. She stopped short and glanced around her. She must have taken a wrong turning. She felt sure she'd never been in this chamber before.

Damn! There was nothing for it but to retrace her steps. She turned around impatiently, but, at that very moment, like a hand blotting out the sun, her torch went out.

For a moment she just stood there, frozen to the spot, as ice-cold panic flickered inside her. It was so silent, so still, here in the bowels of the earth. And as black as pitch, for there were no lights in this little chamber. Suddenly, she couldn't see a thing.

Harriet counted to ten and breathed slowly for a moment. She mustn't panic. Panicking wouldn't help her. But keeping a check on her racing heart was easier said than done. Her fear was so strong that it was difficult to breathe.

She counted to ten again and began to cross the chamber, gingerly, arms like feelers stretched out in front of her, heading for what she hoped was the entrance she'd come through, which would lead her back to where she ought to be. Through the darkness her eyes strained for a glimmer of light.

But it seemed the further she went, the darker it grew. And the more silent. The only sound was the clamour of her heart.

And that was when, leaning against the wall, fighting back the waves of panic that now threatened to engulf and consume her totally, she opened her mouth and with all the power of her lungs yelled, 'Dexter! Dexter! I'm lost! Please come and find me!'

But that desperate cry for help only served to increase her terror, for her voice had seemed to fall like cotton wool at her feet, muffled by the thick, ancient walls of the chamber. In the thin air not an echo was to be heard.

And suddenly she was close to tears as she tripped and stumbled and groped her way blindly over the uneven floor. Her mouth was dry with fear, her body and limbs trembling.

Was this it? A sob shook her. Was it her fate to be entombed?

CHAPTER FIVE

AND then, as she groped blindly through the darkness, with not the faintest idea of where she was going, suddenly Harriet collided with some unseen object and fell clumsily to the ground, dropping her torch. And she very nearly burst into tears of relief as the torch miraculously switched itself back on!

With a prayer of thanks, she snatched it up. 'I'm saved!' she breathed, clutching it tight.

Then she frowned as something caught her eye. A small, glistening object, half hidden behind a rock. Curious, she bent to pick it up.

It was a pendant, made of gold and set with lapis lazuli, about two and a half inches long, in the shape of an ankh, the ancient Egyptian symbol of good luck and long life. Harriet held it in her hand and looked down at it in wonder. This must have belonged to King Horthot, she suddenly realised. This beautiful object must be thousands of years old!

She clasped it in her hand, savouring a sense of pure elation. So, the tomb robbers hadn't got away with everything, after all!

But almost in the same instant her sense of elation withered. What good was the ankh to her if she and it were destined to remain lost here forever in this ancient pharaoh's tomb? Feeling her fear once more creep up on her, semi-distractedly, she thrust the ankh into her bag. And it was at that precise moment that her torch went out again.

'Oh, no! I don't believe it!' Violently, she shook it. 'Please switch on again!' she begged into the darkness. Without the torch, what hope did she have of finding her way?

None whatsoever, it very quickly became plain to her, as she proceeded to stagger through seemingly endless darkness. She was getting nowhere. She'd lost all sense of direction. And, for all she knew, with each step she took she was moving further and further in the wrong direction, deeper and deeper into the caves, so deep that nobody would ever find her.

She fell to her knees. 'Dexter!' she wailed. 'For God's sake, Dexter, come and find me!'

'Harriet!'

The cry seemed to come from a long way off, and for one startled moment Harriet thought she had imagined it. But as she raised her head in hope, she heard it again, more clearly.

'Harriet! Harriet! Where are you, Harriet?'

Instantly, breathlessly, she was scrambling to her feet and rushing headlong in the direction of the voice. 'Dexter! I'm here! I'm here!' she was yelling.

And then she saw the light, dimly, shifting, as he moved his torch from side to side. Harriet's heart swelled inside her. She was safe, after all! She darted towards the light with a cry of gratitude, turned a corner, and went careering straight into him.

'What the devil have you been up to?' All at once his arms were round her, holding her against him, his fingers firm against her back. His voice was gruff as he demanded, scowling down at her, 'Have you any idea what a scare you gave me?'

'What about the scare I gave myself?' Harriet smiled weakly as she leaned against him. 'I thought I was dead. I thought I was lost for good.'

'I was beginning to think the same.' His hands stroked her back. 'What the devil happened? Where is your torch?'

'My torch packed up. That was the problem. I took a wrong turning, and then another one. I hadn't a clue where I was going.' Her voice broke and a shiver went through her suddenly as the immensity of the relief she felt overwhelmed her. 'I really did believe that I was done for.'

'There was no danger of that. Not as long as I'm around.' He held her close for a moment, his arms tight around her. 'If I'd had to tear the caves apart I would have found you.' He reached with one finger to brush away a tear that had spilled on to her cheek without her even knowing it. Then he smiled. 'But I confess you gave me a hell of a fright.'

Harriet looked up into his face and saw that he meant it. The jet-black eyes, normally so arrogant and uncaring, were clouded now with undisguised emotion. There was real concern there, genuine relief. He really had been worried—not just angry, as she might have expected. And he was making no attempt whatsoever to hide it.

It was in that moment, as she looked at him, that two things happened. All at once, she became aware of the hard heat of his body, pressing against her, making her skin tingle. And simultaneously she realised, with a sense of strange excitement, that

Dexter Ross was not the man of constrained emotions that he had led her to believe he was.

He was quite the opposite. He was a man who felt deeply and intensely all manner of fierce and turbulent passions.

A shiver went through her. A shiver of sudden longing. A longing to unlock those powerful, secret passions and drown in the depths of those sinfully black eyes.

What madness! These were thoughts of an unbalanced mind, a mind thrown into disarray by her recent trauma. As she continued to stand there, looking up at him, Harriet tried to cast these strange thoughts and longings from her. This is Dexter Ross, she reminded herself, and I hate him. But still she did not move away.

The hands against her back seemed to burn through her blouse and the hard, muscular chest that pressed lightly against her breasts was turning her flesh to helpless jelly. She could smell the clean scent of him. It filled her nostrils. And she imagined she could feel the warmth of the lips that hovered now inches from her hair-line. As her eyes flickered to those lips, something squeezed inside her.

'I see you found your bag. So at least your journey wasn't wasted.' He was smiling down at her, a wry, self-mocking smile. 'The whole thing's my fault. I should have come with you.'

'No, you shouldn't. I told you not to.'

'I shouldn't have listened. I should have insisted. After all, I knew you were upset.'

'Upset?' For a moment, Harriet failed to comprehend him. Then as his expression subtly altered, as though a dark veil had fallen, she remembered her silly outburst about Tom. 'That was nothing,' she protested. 'I wasn't really upset.'

'You seemed upset to me.' He spoke softly, watching her. Then he drew back a little. 'I suggest we talk about this later.'

'No!' Harriet held on to him. 'Let's talk about it now.' She might never have another moment of such closeness between them, when she could feel, almost tangibly, her power to bend his will.

She looked up into his face. 'I got lost because my torch went out. Anyone would have got lost in that situation. It had nothing to do with what happened earlier.' She took a deep breath, feeling her heart beat inside her. 'You must believe that. I can do the job you need me for.'

There was a long moment's silence, as Dexter stood there looking down at her, and she could tell that there were all sorts of thoughts flying through his head, just as there were flying through her own, and that the question of her job-worthiness was only one of them.

Then he drew away from her gently and nodded his head. 'OK,' he conceded. 'I'll give you one more chance!'

It was only later, after the day's work was completed and they'd had lunch at the hotel, then gone off to their separate rooms, that Harriet remembered about the ankh.

She'd been thinking about Dexter and all that had passed between them after he'd found her down in the cave.

Her cheeks flushed as she remembered the physical longing that had torn through her as he'd held her in his arms. The way her flesh had seemed to melt. The way her blood had burned. The silly way her head had spun.

What would it have been like, she wondered, if he had kissed me?

She pushed the thought away. Though she sensed he had come close, he had not kissed her. And she was glad.

Glad, she told herself, for a dozen different reasons. She did not like him. She did not want him. And, as she knew, he already had a girlfriend.

Still, the intensity of her reactions to him worried her a little, until it occurred to her that it was really all very easily explained.

She'd reacted as she had because she'd just had a bad scare. She had already been in a state of high emotion when she'd found herself clasped in Dexter's arms. And she'd been grateful. That was why all her hostility to him had vanished. It was only to be expected that one should feel positively towards someone who had just taken the trouble to save one's life!

And he'd seemed different, too. That had been a part of it.

Harriet shook her head. He'd seemed different, but he wasn't. If he'd been relieved to see her, if he'd been thrown a little off balance, that was only to be expected, too. Think of the trouble it would have caused him if she'd vanished without trace!

No, she decided, none of her feelings for him had changed. She still disliked him. She still disapproved of him. She still had nothing but total contempt for his selfish, grasping philosophy of life that allowed him to care for no one but himself, and that reminded her so vividly of Tom. She had been taken in once. She would not be taken in again.

Harriet's lips pursed disapprovingly. Money and possessions were the only things that Dexter cared about. And his priceless collection of Egyptian antiquities, she suspected, meant more than anything else.

That was when she remembered.

She sat up with a start, as suddenly, in her mind's eye, she saw the dusty gold ankh that she'd found in the tomb, slipped into her bag and then forgotten all about. She leapt from her seat, grabbed her bag, and reached inside it.

And there it was. Harriet held it in her hand and gazed down at it in wonderment for a moment. Then with a tissue she gently wiped away the dust, so that the pale gold shone and the blue lapis lazuli glistened as though it were newly polished. A sudden thought went through her. How Dexter would love it!

Her fingers closed round it, almost protectively. And in that moment she made herself a promise. Dexter would never have it. He would never add it to his collection!

Ten minutes later she was leaving her room, the pendant once more in her bag, carefully wrapped in a cocoon of tissues. Until she had decided what to do with it she must keep it somewhere safe, and the safest place that she could think of was a safety deposit box in the strong-room at hotel reception.

A cold shiver touched her as she hurried past Dexter's door. He was not the wisest man to choose as one's enemy. With those who crossed him he would have no mercy—and she would be done for if he ever found out what she was doing.

She crossed her fingers. So he must never find out.

As the days passed Harriet realised Dexter hadn't been joking. Acting as his assistant was no doddle. The hours she worked were long and the work was tiring.

She and Dexter would spend all morning in the tomb, then, after lunch and a short siesta, she'd spend several hours at her desk typing up Dexter's dictated notes.

But Harriet had no complaints. She found the work absorbing. She was even, in a way, enjoying working with Dexter.

He knew so much. He had endless, fascinating stories to recount about the history of the tombs. And Harriet loved to listen to these stories. It was like being invited to share a whole new world.

She was also witnessing a whole new side to Dexter Ross.

In the tomb, once he became absorbed in what he was doing, all his harshness seemed to drop away. Sometimes Harriet would find herself slanting a look at him, as he bent over some particularly intricate piece of work, and the thought would occur to her that one could almost imagine that behind those handsome dark-eyed features beat a normal human heart, capable of compassion and caring.

On those occasions she came very close to liking him.

But she knew the mask he wore at work was deceptive. Though he was not the cold creature she had once believed he was—he was a man of strong passions, she was still very sure of that—the passions that consumed him would be selfish and self-serving. He only cared for himself. He had no feelings for others. And there was no fear of her forgetting for there were constant reminders.

She bumped into him in the corridor one evening on her way down to the dining-room. Over one shoulder he was carrying a rolled-up carpet.

'Been shopping, I see?' She glanced curiously at the carpet. On her one brief visit to the local bazaar she had seen some of the beautiful carpets that were on sale there. Had she been able to afford it, she would have bought one herself!

Dexter had paused in mid-stride. 'It's to add to my collection. I have quite a few carpets that I've bought when I've been over here.'

So, he collected carpets as well as antiquities! Was there no end to this man's greedy acquisitiveness?

Harriet narrowed her eyes at him. 'How nice for you,' she told him, and was about to walk past him when he added,

'You'll be happy to hear I got it for a very good price.'

It was the way he sounded so pleased with himself that really grated. Harriet paused and flicked him a cool look. 'Yes, I'm sure you did.'

'In fact, I got it for about half of what the shopkeeper originally asked. Really a very good price indeed.'

He was needling her deliberately. It amused him to see her angry. Out of control of her emotions, as he would call it.

Harriet looked straight at him, her dark eyes with disapproval, but, for all that, perfectly in control. 'That doesn't surprise me. I know you're an expert haggler. Remember, I've had the privilege of seeing you in action.'

Dexter smiled and shifted the carpet more comfortably across his shoulder. 'I take it you're referring to my negotiations with our taxi drivers?'

Negotiations, he called them! How about that for a euphemism? 'Yes, that was precisely what I was referring to.'

'But they're quite happy with our arrangement. So, why on earth should you complain?'

Harriet knew what he was getting at. The same two taxi drivers—Omar, who drove them between the hotel and the ferry, and Mohamed, who did the trip from the ferry to the Valley of the Kings—had continued to look after them every day throughout their stay. That might appear to indicate that they were content with the deal.

On the other hand, there could be a very different reason. Harriet proceeded to put it to him now.

'They don't complain, I imagine, because you provide them with regular work. And regular work is better than no work, even when it's badly paid. They're better off accepting the pittance you offer them than they would be if they were just waiting around for customers.'

'So, I'm doing them a good turn? Even you agree?' He smiled, amused at his own cleverness, as he said it.

'You'd be doing them a better turn if you paid them a bit more.'

'And because I can afford to, you think I ought to?'

'As a matter of fact I do.' Harriet nodded at that carpet slung carelessly across his shoulder. 'Did you ever stop to think how many hours of labour went into the making of a carpet like that? Dozens of hours. Possibly even hundreds. And yet all you can think of,' she concluded tartly, 'is how clever you were to have knocked the shopkeeper down to half his original price.'

'Not quite half. It was slightly over.' He smiled a shameless, unrepentant smile. 'I wasn't quite as clever as you're making out.'

Their eyes met and locked, his filled with sheer arrogance, hers bright with angry disapproval.

Then, with a final amused smile, he proceeded to sweep past her. 'I'm going to my room now to admire my new carpet.'

Harriet turned to glare after him. He really was despicable! But as she hurried downstairs, a new thought occurred to her that caused a smile to light up her eyes.

While he was enjoying his new carpet, little did he know that downstairs, locked inside her safe-box, was a treasure he would trade a wagonload of carpets for—and that he would never get his greedy hands near. The priceless gold and lapis ankh!

Down in the dining-room, as the waiter came and took her order, Harriet's thoughts continued to focus on the ankh. Over the past few days she'd tried to put it from her mind. Thinking about it made her nervous. But now, thanks to this latest boost to her antipathy for him, she was suddenly in the mood for plotting against Dexter.

And time was passing, after all. More than a week had gone by since she'd found the pendant. It was time she had some idea what she intended to do with it. She couldn't leave it in her safety deposit box for ever.

She glanced out of the window and over the terrace, past the shrubbery of the gardens, towards the moonlit Nile. And suddenly an idea that had been forming in her head seemed to crystallise into perfect clarity. Suddenly she knew what she must do to ensure that Dexter never laid a hand on that ankh.

And she would not wait. She would make her first move tomorrow.

'Are you feeling all right? You're very quiet.'

Harriet glanced up with a nervous start as Dexter spoke suddenly. 'I'm feeling fine,' she answered quickly, forcing the sort of bright smile that someone who was feeling fine would smile. Then she added, fearing he might have seen through her smile's falseness, 'Perhaps I'm just a little tired.'

'Getting to you, is it? The pace, I mean? Is this the first sign that you're about to fall by the wayside?'

'Definitely not!' This time Harriet's response was honest. If she'd been quieter than usual while they'd been having lunch, it was not because she was feeling poorly. The reason was something else entirely.

They'd got back from the tombs, as usual, just after one, and were sitting in the hotel dining-room having lunch together—though Harriet would have preferred to eat in her room. The only reason she hadn't was to avoid arousing suspicion.

For having lunch together had become a habit. It was virtually the only non-working time they ever spent together, and usually, surprisingly, the atmosphere was pleasant. Usually Harriet enjoyed their lunches.

The reason for that, she'd decided, was very simple. For one thing, they tended to talk only about work—and Dexter's mellow mood, which always descended on him while he was working, hadn't quite had time to wear off!

Today, however, Harriet was feeling nervy. Her mind was filled with secret plans and she was finding it hard to concentrate on anything else.

But now, at last, the meal was almost over. As the waiter came to clear away their fruit plates, she glanced across at Dexter. 'I think I'll skip coffee.'

'OK by me. If you're feeling tired, you go ahead and have your siesta.'

That was the routine. Lunch, then siesta. Only, today, a siesta was the last thing on Harriet's mind. For today she was about to take the first step in acting out her little plot.

Excitement rippled through her as she took the lift up to her room. This afternoon she was planning to phone Luxor museum and make an appointment to meet its director. If anyone could advise her what procedure to follow to ensure that the ankh ended up where it belonged—in a public museum in Egypt—he, undoubtedly, was the man.

Though, of course, she reminded herself, as she slipped into her room, she must be careful not to reveal at this point the existence of the ankh. Their discussion must be conducted on a strictly hypothetical level—what would one do if one were lucky enough to find such a treasure?—for once her secret was out that would be that. It would be only a matter of time before Dexter found out.

The museum, she had discovered, didn't open till five. Since it was now just before three, she had two hours to kill. She proceeded to do so by pacing the floor, glancing at her watch every few minutes, rehearsing what she would say when she spoke to the director.

But at last her watch showed five o'clock precisely. She picked up the phone and dialled the museum number, then waited, her heart beating, as it rang.

Five minutes later, satisfied, she laid the phone down again. The director was in Cairo, but she had spoken to his assistant and made an appointment to see the director tomorrow at five.

She rolled back on the bed and laughed out loud with pleasure.

'Dexter Ross, eat your heart out! You'll never know till it's too late what you came so close to having!'

In spite of these pleasant thoughts, Harriet slept badly that night.

She dragged herself out of bed at six the next morning, feeling not a glimmer of her customary enthusiasm. It's the worry, she told herself, of having the ankh in my possession. I won't feel happy until I've found out what I ought to do with it.

But at least she wouldn't have to wait long to find that out. This afternoon at five she'd be seeing the museum director.

Dexter noticed her weary look when they met as usual down in the lobby.

'You look awful,' he told her frankly. 'Are you feeling OK?'

'I feel fine. Just a little tired.' She'd tried to pull herself together. 'I didn't sleep too well, that's all,' she told him.

'No?' One eyebrow lifted. 'So, what kept you from sleeping? Do you have something on your mind?'

'On my mind? No.' A guilty flush touched her cheeks. Was he a wizard, the way he could see inside her head?

'Are you sure?'

'Quite sure.' Harriet shifted her gaze. 'Quite sure,' she repeated. 'I have nothing on my mind.'

He continued to look at her, as though he knew she was lying. 'Nothing?' he queried, making her heart flutter. Then he narrowed his eyes at her. 'Let's hope this isn't a relapse. Regrettably, that would oblige me to take certain measures.'

'A relapse?' Harriet frowned, then belatedly understood. He thought it was her broken heart that was keeping her awake! 'Of course not,' she assured him quickly. 'You have nothing to worry about. I'll be carrying out my duties with my usual efficiency.'

And she did, even though it just about killed her. By the time they were packing up, just before one o'clock, and climbing into the taxi on the first leg back to Luxor, Harriet was starting to feel as though she might collapse at any minute.

This is ridiculous, she told herself, as she slumped gratefully into the back seat. All I did was lose a few hours' sleep. I shouldn't be feeling as exhausted as this!

But she did, and she felt quite unable to tackle lunch. As they stepped through the hotel doors, she was just about to say as much to Dexter when all thoughts of lunch—and anything else—were abruptly evicted from her head.

For, walking towards them across the lobby, was Dexter's girlfriend.

'Dexter!'

'*Habibi*!'

There followed a warm embrace—which Harriet found herself observing with unexpected irritation.

It's because I'm dying to get to my bed, she told herself. I've no wish to waste time hanging around here watching Dexter with his false displays of affection.

Not that he looked at all false; she had to grant him that. He looked as convincing as he had sounded with that greeting, '*Habibi*!', which Harriet just happened to know meant 'my dear'. And his girlfriend quite clearly wasn't acting.

Poor thing, Harriet thought fleetingly, as the girl and Dexter disengaged themselves and the girl turned towards her with a polite smile. I'm sure she has no idea what she's got into.

'You must be Harriet. I'm Nabila.' The girl held out her hand to her. 'I'm pleased to meet you.'

'And I'm pleased to meet you.' Harriet offered her own hand. Poor thing, she thought again, as they shook hands briefly. For, as she looked into the girl's face, she could see that she'd been right in the assessment she'd made that first time she'd glimpsed her. Nabila was far too good for Dexter.

Her beautiful, gentle face betrayed a sensitive, loving nature. Those huge, trusting eyes of hers were full of warmth and kindness. Dexter Ross had no right to be trifling with such a girl.

As though in defiance of this judgement, Dexter was now standing with one hand placed lightly around Nabila's waist. He was saying to her, 'Just give me fifteen minutes to shower and change, then I'll be ready to take you off to lunch.'

'Will Harriet be joining us?' Nabila glanced in Harriet's direction, but the words were scarcely out before Dexter put in quickly,

'No, Harriet won't be joining us. She isn't feeling too well.' He glanced at Harriet. 'Am I right?'

'Absolutely right.' Illogically, she felt offended. It went through her head with a sense of silly disappointment that not only was she being deprived of her usual enjoyable lunch with Dexter, but into the bargain she was being summarily packed off to bed!

Which is precisely, she reminded herself sharply, what I want! Hadn't she already decided she was incapable of lunch and that all she desired was to climb into bed?

She pulled herself together. 'Dexter's absolutely right. I am feeling a little under the weather.' She took a step back. 'So, if you don't mind, I'll leave you.' She smiled quickly at Nabila. 'Enjoy your lunch.'

Then she turned and walked smartly across the lobby to the lift.

Up in her room Harriet flopped down on the bed. Roll on this afternoon! she thought, staring at the ceiling. Roll on my appointment with the museum director! Worrying about that ankh is making me crazy. It even appears to be affecting my judgement about Dexter! For a moment back then I was actually *sorry* that I wouldn't be having lunch with him today!

She rolled over and closed her eyes. What I need is forty winks. That should help to get my head back together again!

But in fact, though she slept, it was not a soothing sleep. It was a sleep filled with vivid, frightening dreams. Harriet dreamed she went to her deposit box and discovered the ankh was missing. She awoke with a start, beaded in sweat.

And though she knew it was illogical, she was suddenly filled with panic. Could the dream be true? Was the ankh no longer in her locker?

She knew it made no sense, but the fear refused to leave her. There was nothing else for it. She had to check.

It was just after four-thirty when she hurried down to the lobby, feeling as though her brain were on fire. She would check her locker before taking a taxi to the museum.

Her legs were rubbery with anxiety; she felt almost dizzy with apprehension, in spite of what her common sense was telling her. It was impossible that the ankh had gone missing from her locker. But she had to know for sure. She approached the reception desk.

'I need something from my deposit box,' she told the young man on duty.

A moment later she was being led to the reinforced room where all the safety deposit boxes were kept, watching as the receptionist released her locker then laid it down on a nearby table.

Harriet crossed to the table and, with heavy, trembling fingers, lifted the lid, hardly daring to look inside. But then she gasped. There was the ankh, still in its wrapper of tissues! Relief poured through her as she reached out to pick it up, clasping it in her hand, finally reassured.

But at that very moment the locker-room door opened.

As a voice spoke, a voice she recognized instantly, she whirled round and felt her heart stand still inside her. Suddenly, aghast, she was looking into Dexter's sharp black eyes.

A rush of panic tore through her. And that was all she remembered. The dizziness in her head seemed to be pulling her under. Her rubbery legs could no longer support her. Suddenly everything went black as she fell to the floor.

She was only vaguely aware of Dexter scooping her from the floor and carrying her upstairs to her room. But as he laid her on the bed, just before she drifted off again, with perfect clarity she heard him say, 'What a pity. Now you won't be able to keep your appointment at the museum.'

CHAPTER SIX

'DON'T worry, Miss Kaye. In a couple of days you'll be fine. A bug, that's all it is. Nothing serious. These pills I've prescribed will soon clear it up.'

Harriet was sitting up in bed, propped against a pile of pillows and already feeling a great deal better. She smiled a grateful smile at the kind-faced doctor. 'Thank you for coming to see me so quickly.'

The doctor smiled back at her, then glanced across at Dexter, who, throughout the consultation, had remained in the room with them. 'Mr Ross's call came just as I was finishing my ward round at the clinic. So, I got in my car and came straight over.'

Harriet resisted the urge to follow the doctor's gaze. Since she had regained consciousness she had scarcely dared to look at Dexter. Every time she even thought of him she remembered those chilling words he had spoken as he'd laid her on the bed. 'What a pity. Now you won't be able to keep your appointment at the museum.'

Her blood ran cold. How did he know about her appointment? And did he know also what the purpose of it had been?

There was another question, too, that she scarcely dared think of. What had happened to the ankh?

Harriet's stomach clenched fearfully now as Dexter spoke. 'I'll get someone from the hotel to go to the pharmacy and get Dr Fahmy's prescription right away.' He crossed to the phone at the side of her bed, punched in a number, then spoke rapidly in Arabic. Then, laying down the receiver, he paused to look down at Harriet. 'Dr Fahmy is the finest doctor in Luxor. You can take his word for it; you'll soon be back on your feet.'

'I'm feeling better already.' She dared to glance at him quickly, wishing he would move away from the side of the bed. His nearness was making it difficult for her to breathe. 'I'm sorry I passed out on you downstairs like that.'

'I wasn't altogether surprised.' The dark eyes fixed her. 'I could see since morning you weren't feeling too great. I just wish you'd come out and admitted it earlier, then I could have called Dr Fahmy at once.'

'I thought I was just tired.'

Harriet glanced away guiltily. More accurately, she'd believed that her symptoms were being caused by her anxious, near panicky state of mind. The fire in her head, the weakness in her limbs she had attributed to the fierce inner turmoil that gripped her. It had been a relief, in a way, to discover that the culprit was nothing more sinister that a simple tummy bug. She'd been starting to think she was becoming neurotic!

'Never mind. She'll be fine now.' Dr Fahmy was speaking. 'These tummy bugs are very common. It's the change of diet that does it, combined with the unaccustomed heat and dust. But if you take the pills I've prescribed you shouldn't have any more problems.'

He glanced at Dexter, who was still standing by the bedside. 'Of course, if there are any more problems, you'll get in touch at once.'

'Of course.' Dexter nodded and smiled in response. Then, as Fahmy prepared to leave, he laid a hand on the doctor's shoulder and added something in Arabic that caused him to laugh.

Quite evidently, Harriet observed, the two knew each other well. Perhaps Fahmy was the doctor who had attended to her predecessor, Dexter's regular assistant, who'd had to be flown home. Somehow it was beyond the bounds of imagination that Dexter himself had ever been his patient. Dexter Ross was made of steel. Both his body and his soul.

That was not a reassuring thought. As the doctor bade her farewell, Harriet's eyes drifted fearfully in Dexter's direction. Would he now send her home as well?

But that fear was still a small one compared to the others that filled her head. How had Dexter known about her appointment at the museum? And what had happened to the ankh?

The doctor had gone now and the door was closing behind him. Harriet felt her stomach shrink as Dexter turned towards her. Were all the questions she dared not ask him now about to be answered? Was she about to be subjected to the full force of his wrath?

But all he said was, 'I've arranged for the doctor to hand in the prescription at Reception. As I said, someone from the hotel will go and fetch it. It should be with us within half an hour.'

'Good.' Harriet nodded. Her mouth was as dry as paper. 'Thank you,' she added. 'You've been most helpful.'

To anyone else she would have said kind. But kindness was not an attribute she felt capable of associating with Dexter. 'Helpful' was the most positive description she could manage.

'No need for thanks.' He continued to watch her as he stood there between the door and the bed, his hands thrust casually into his trouser pockets. 'I could scarcely have left you lying on the strong-room floor. Apart from anything else, you were blocking the door.'

He smiled as he said it, a smile that surprised her. The last thing she'd been expecting was a display of good humour. She smiled back a little nervously. 'How inconsiderate of me,' she said.

'I don't know about inconsiderate, but it was certainly pretty dramatic. I walked in to get some traveller's cheques out of my deposit box... You turned round, took one look at me, and fell in a faint to the floor.' He smiled again. 'I don't usually have that effect on people. Now I know how Dracula must feel.'

This time, as Harriet smiled back at him, she felt her nervousness dissolve. Whatever he knew, whatever he had decided, he was not about to confront her with it now. For the moment at least it would be safe to relax.

She shook her head. 'I really had no idea I was ill. Thank you for organising the doctor and everything.'

Dexter shrugged. 'As I said, there's no need for thanks. I simply did what had to be done. I am, after all, responsible for your welfare.'

'Are you?'

The question was a reflex action. The notion of anyone other than herself being responsible for her welfare was new and strange to her. Since she'd left her mother's home at the age of eighteen, Harriet had grown accustomed to standing on her own two feet.

'I think so. You're here because of me. You're in a strange country. Of course I'm responsible for you.'

Harriet looked back at him, not quite certain how to respond. Part of her wanted to protest. She was no poor, helpless female in need of some man to look out for her welfare—in spite of fainting in the strong-room and getting lost in the caves! But part of her, she had to confess, felt oddly reassured. For instinctively she sensed that, if one had to choose a protector, there would be few men better equipped for the role than Dexter.

What was it he had said to her when he'd come to her rescue in the caves? That she'd been in no real danger as long as he was around? That he'd have torn the caves apart in order to find her?

Remembering that as she looked at him now, a warm glow spread through her. How wonderful to have such strength and determination to rely on.

Then she shook herself in horror. This bug was making her brain soft! She could rely on nothing from Dexter Ross, and nor did she have the slightest wish to do so! Besides, his strength and determination that had filled her momentarily with such admiration would be born of a sense of duty, not compassion. There was nothing particularly wonderful about that!

'I'll leave you now.' He was turning to go. 'As soon as the prescription arrives I'll bring it in to you, then you can stay in bed for the rest of the day. According to Dr Fahmy, by tomorrow you'll be feeling better. You'll probably feel like getting up...'

He paused, and smiled an inscrutable smile. 'But, alas, you won't be up to working...'

Was this it? The axe blow she'd been fearing? Harriet stiffened anxiously. 'I expect not,' she began, 'but——'

'That's unfortunate. It means——'

'But I'll soon be better!' Before he could finish, Harriet broke in. 'Dr Fahmy said so! In a couple of days I'll be fit enough for work!'

Dexter raised black eyebrows. 'Are you so keen to get back to work, then?'

'Absolutely.' Harriet raised herself from the pillows. 'And it wouldn't make sense for you to fire me and bring in my replacement—if that's what you're thinking of doing,' she added defensively. 'Dr Fahmy said I should have no more problems.' She leaned towards him urgently and argued, 'If you were to bring in my replacement, she might fall ill, too—after all, this tummy bug is very common—and you would simply end up losing even more time.

'So, you see,' she concluded, 'it makes sense to keep me on. It would be silly to risk bringing in someone new now.'

Dexter allowed a silence to fall as she came to the end of her entreaty. Unhurriedly, his eyes scanned her flushed, anxious face. Then he told her, 'I had already reached that conclusion myself. What I was about to say before you interrupted me was that your temporary indisposition probably means that we may have to stay on an extra couple of days. I hope that won't be inconvenient?'

'No, not in the slightest.' Harriet fell back with relief. 'I can stay on as long as you like.'

Dexter smiled and held her eyes. 'So, on that point you can relax.' Then, as he was about to leave the room, he paused for a moment, and added in a tone that caused her heart to tighten, 'I can assure you I have not the slightest intention of releasing you.'

What did that mean? Harriet shivered as the door closed behind him. It sounded as though he was planning something. Something, she sensed, she was not going to like.

She thought again of his remark about her museum appointment, and of the ankh, whose fate remained a mystery. Did he know about it? Had it fallen from her hand when she fainted? Was he just waiting till she was stronger before turning his anger on her?

She lay rigid for a moment, her heart thundering inside her. Perhaps, after all, it might have been better if he had dismissed her and put her on the first plane back to England!

Then a thought crossed her mind. If he already had the ankh—if she had dropped it and he had picked it up—wasn't that precisely what he would do? Get her out of the way and hang on to his booty?

So, perhaps he didn't have it. Suddenly, her brain was whirring. Perhaps it had rolled out of sight into some corner.

Or perhaps...

Her eyes lit up with sudden hope. She sprang from the bed and flung herself across the room to the chair where she had noticed earlier her bag was lying. Then she pulled the flap open and thrust her hand inside, feeling her heart nearly stop inside her chest as her fingers made contact with a small, hard object, carefully wrapped in a cocoon of tissues.

Harriet pulled it out and gazed at it, tears of relief in her eyes. She must have acted automatically, just before she passed out. Though she certainly hadn't been aware of doing it, she must have quickly slipped the ankh into her bag.

She closed her hand around it and put up a prayer of thanks. The worst, after all, had not happened. The ankh hadn't fallen into Dexter's hands. He still didn't even know of its existence!

She slipped it back into her bag and returned to her bed. Now all she had to do was invent some reason to explain away her appointment with the museum director. For sooner or later Dexter would confront her with that. And when he did, she must make certain she was prepared.

She smiled to herself. That shouldn't be too difficult. Then she sank against the pillows. She was saved!

Over the next twenty-four hours, Dexter was the very essence of thoughtfulness.

He brought Harriet's medicine to her and watched over her while she took it. He organised room service to provide her with specially prepared light meals—for her stomach still felt a little delicate. He produced books for her to read and a pile of videos for her to choose from. It seemed there was nothing he was not more than willing to do for her.

And not one solitary uncivil word passed between them. How charming—even likeable!—he could be when he tried.

As predicted, by the following afternoon Harriet was feeling much better, fit enough to get out of bed.

'I think I'll get dressed,' she told Dexter, when he came to supervise her pill taking. 'I fancy going down to sit by the pool for a while.'

'Good idea. I'll come with you.' He glanced at his watch. 'I'll meet you in the lobby in half an hour.'

Drat! 'There's really no need for you to come with me. I'm sure you've better things to do.'

The truth was she'd been hoping to create an opportunity to replace the ankh in her safe deposit box. The thought of carrying it around with her gave her goosebumps and she felt equally nervous about leaving it in her room. But she could scarcely go to the strong-room if Dexter was with her!

She tried to convince him with a smile. 'I'll be all right on my own.'

But he would have none of it. He seemed to be enjoying his role of guardian angel. 'Just over twenty-four hours ago you were fainting at my feet. I wouldn't dream of letting you out on your own.'

The smile that accompanied this protestation caused an odd sensation to catch at Harriet's heart. It reminded her for a flickering instant of the way he'd looked at her in the cave, with that expression of undisguised concern in his eyes.

And though she told herself it was only because he wanted her back at work, deep inside she felt pleased and oddly flattered. He really was taking very good care of her. Perhaps he didn't dislike her totally, after all.

Not, of course, that she cared one jot whether he liked her, she told herself, as she arrived in the lobby half an hour later to find Dexter already there, waiting for her by the fountain. Not one jot, she repeated, as he led her out to the pool.

At this time of day—just after five—the sun was beginning to lose its fierceness and there were quite a few guests lying on sunbeds round the pool. On a word from Dexter the pool attendant found two together, at the shady end of the pool, and spread them with towels.

'*Shokrun.*' Thank you. Dexter handed the man a tip, then beckoned one of the waiters who patrolled the poolside area. As the man approached, he said something else in Arabic.

The waiter nodded, before hurrying off. '*Tayyib.* Right away, sir.'

Harriet sat down on one of the sunbeds, laying her shoulder-bag beside her—hidden inside it was the precious ankh!—and watched Dexter beneath her lashes as he stripped off his shorts and T-shirt before seating himself next to her on the adjacent sunbed. He had the body of a Greek god, she thought a little foolishly. Powerful and sinuous, moulded to perfection. No wonder he moved with such easy, fluid grace.

She was aware, too, with a flare of illogical irritation, that there were many other female eyes besides her own currently enjoying the spectacle of his virile perfection. Yet, to his credit, he seemed sublimely unaware of this admiration—though that was more than likely a façade, Harriet corrected herself quickly. Secretly, he was probably lapping it up!

It was at that moment that the waiter reappeared, carrying a beer and a glass of orange juice. He laid the drinks on the wicker table between the sunbeds and handed Dexter the bill, saying something in Arabic—to which Dexter responded with a smile.

Perhaps to balance her earlier feelings of admiration, Harriet experienced a sudden, welcome spurt of irritation. He was so damned in control. Everyone was so desperate to do his bidding. While some men spent hours gesticulating in vain, all Dexter had to do was simply appear for pool attendants and waiters to materialise at his elbow!

There was a further exchange of pleasantries.

'*Shokrun.*'

'*Afwan.*' Don't mention it.

Then, as the waiter departed, Dexter was turning to her. 'I'm sorry. I ordered orange juice for you without asking what you wanted.' He smiled. 'But I've noticed it's what you usually drink.'

'Orange juice is fine.' It was what she would have ordered, though, perversely, she was wishing she had cause to find fault. Harriet narrowed her eyes at him as she leaned back against her sunbed. One way or another, she *would* find fault. Her feelings towards this man had been growing far too positive!

She turned to him. 'Why do you insist on speaking Arabic to the hotel staff? All of them speak perfectly good English.'

Why do you insist on showing off? That was what she was really saying. And she could see from the way he looked back at her that he had understood perfectly.

But his tone was unruffled as he answered her. 'Don't you think it's polite, when one's in another country, at least to make some attempt to speak that country's language?'

Harriet paused and frowned. She agreed wholeheartedly. It was no less than common courtesy to make some kind of effort to pick up a few words of one's host country's language. Since she'd been in Egypt, she'd even offered the occasional '*shokrun*' herself!

She slid her gaze away. 'I suppose so,' she agreed reluctantly. 'I just think that maybe you overdo it. You could relax from time to time and just speak English.'

Dexter laughed then, surprising her, so that she turned round to look at him. 'Don't worry,' he assured her. 'Speaking Arabic is no effort for me. I've been speaking Arabic as long as I've been speaking English.'

Harriet felt her eyebrows lift.

'My mother was Egyptian. At home we spoke both Arabic and English.'

'Your mother was Egyptian?'

'Yes. From Cairo.'

'Good grief.' Harriet stared at him, feeling suddenly foolish. She ought to have guessed, she found herself thinking. Those midnight-black eyes of his and that raven-dark hair were very definitely not English! 'I'd no idea,' she offered. It was all she could think of to say.

'How could you?' He smiled a tolerant smile. 'After all, I don't have hieroglyphics tattooed on my forehead.'

Harriet smiled back at him in spite of herself. 'No, you don't. But at least now I know where your love of Egyptology comes from.' She remembered him saying he'd been interested in it since childhood. Suddenly, one or two small mysteries were starting to make sense.

Dexter smiled. 'My maternal grandfather was a keen Egyptologist. When I was a child and we used to come to Egypt on holiday, he would take me with him when he went on expeditions. He was the one who really got me hooked.'

A glow of warmth went through her and Harriet smiled fondly as the sudden touching image of a dark-haired little boy, walking hand in hand across the sand-dunes with his grandfather, suddenly flashed across her mind. What a beautiful, bright-eyed child he must have been.

But instantly these feeling shocked her. She thrust them from her, drew herself back against her sunbed and said as matter-of-factly as she could, 'You were lucky. I never really knew my grandparents.'

'How come?'

'Circumstances. My father died when I was two and my mother unfortunately lost touch with his family. And both her own parents were already dead.'

'That's a shame.'

'I know. It's something I've always regretted.' She allowed herself to relax a little again and look at him. 'I would love to have had at least one doting grandparent.'

'I suppose I had four, and I suppose I took them all for granted. I was an only child. I'm sure I was spoiled rotten.' Dexter caught her eye and smiled at her wickedly. 'But, as I'm sure you'll agree, it didn't do me any harm.'

Harriet was grateful for the opportunity to utter a small ironical laugh. It helped to reduce the tension inside her.

She said, without malice, 'I might have guessed you were an only child.'

'I take it you're not?' His eyes looked back at her, amused.

'I have a sister, a year younger than me.' Harriet smiled proudly. 'She's a high-powered secretary. She lives in London.'

'And is your mother still alive?'

'Oh, yes. Alive and flourishing. She lives in Reigate. I see her quite often.' She paused. 'I take it your mother is dead?'

He nodded. 'Yes. My mother died some years ago.'

'I'm sorry to hear that. She must have been quite young?'

'Young enough.' He swivelled round to face the swimming-pool. 'Certainly much too young to die.'

There was something in his tone that caused Harriet's heart to flicker, almost with a sense of guilt. Unwittingly, she sensed, she had touched a raw spot.

She was about to lean towards him and offer an apology for dwelling on a subject that was obviously painful. But before she could say a word, he was rising to his feet and pushing her orange juice towards her.

'Drink up,' he told her. 'I'm going for a swim.'

A moment later he was diving from the pool edge, cutting the aquamarine water as cleanly as a knife. More perfection, Harriet observed, but without annoyance. On the contrary, she was aware of a wave of sympathy, coupled with a sense of bewildered surprise. For the first time he had, indisputably, shown a human face.

As he'd talked about his grandfather and his dead mother there had been real human affection—and loss—in the dark eyes.

Harriet watched him now as he scythed through the clear blue water, causing barely a ripple as his strong arms propelled him forward. In a way it was reassuring to know he was capable of such feelings, yet, inexplicably, more than reassured she felt unsettled by this new knowledge. He'd somehow slipped through the net of what she'd believed him to be.

But had he? As he executed a perfect turn and proceeded with ease to do a second length of the pool, Harriet focused on the hard core of disapproval deep inside her.

What he'd just revealed to her simply made his crimes more disgraceful. The fact that he himself was half Egyptian made his greedy appropriation of his collection of Egyptian artefacts even more contemptible than she had first judged it to be. He of all people should appreciate that these things belonged in Egypt!

As he turned again and began a third, effortless length of the pool, Harriet was already starting to feel a lot less unsettled. The sympathy he had aroused in her was melting away.

Think, too, she reminded herself, of Omar and Mohamed, the two taxi drivers—and the carpet seller—whom he had treated so shabbily. He was rich beyond the dreams of any of these people—rich beyond the dreams of most mortal men!—yet he grudged paying them a single penny more than he could get away with.

And they were *his* people! That made it even more shameful! If he had any real decency he ought to be trying to help them.

She had lost count of the number of lengths he had done now. The taut, powerful body moved like a perfectly oiled machine, tirelessly, exquisitely, through the limpid water. And that was what he was, Harriet decided with a sense of satisfaction. An exquisite, uncaring, perfect machine.

OK, so, after all, there were some things that could touch him. But the harsh truth of what he was remained.

While she dwelt on these thoughts, she had failed to notice that he had swum to the edge, right in front of her, and was lifting himself out of the water in one smooth movement. Then he was rising to his feet and stepping towards her, a muscular, black-haired, dripping Adonis.

As she looked up and caught sight of him, Harriet felt her heart turn over. Just for an instant her blood leapt in her veins.

Antipathy, she told herself, knowing it was nothing of the sort. It was that dangerous physical reaction to him that she was unable to control and for which she despised herself from the bottom of her heart. Knowing what he was, she should be immune.

'That's better.' He was flopping down on the sunbed beside her, giving his hair a quick rub with the towel. Then he glanced across at her. 'Are you still feeling OK? You're not finding the heat too much, I hope?'

'I'm feeling perfectly fine.' But suddenly that wasn't true. All at once she found his nearness unsettling.

Harriet rose to her feet and peeled off her sundress to reveal the bikini she was wearing underneath. 'I think I'll just have a quick dip myself.'

Then with a sense of huge relief that she knew was silly she stepped to the edge of the pool and jumped in.

Harriet stayed for about fifteen minutes in the water, swimming lazily, floating on her back, gazing up at the huge expanse of clear blue sky, resolutely banishing the unsettling feeling that Dexter had so unexpectedly stirred in her. By the time she climbed out and headed back to her sunbed, she was feeling refreshed, both mentally and physically.

Then, as her gaze fell on her sunbed, she stopped in her tracks.

She felt her mouth drop open.

Where was her bag?

Dexter was sitting watching her. He leaned towards her slightly. 'What's the matter? You look as though you've seen a ghost.'

The way Harriet's heart was beating it was difficult to speak. She looked at Dexter, then once again at the empty space where her bag had been, and a thousand fearful thoughts went racing through her head. How could she have gone off like that and forgotten all about it?

She licked her suddenly dry lips. 'Where's my bag?' she said at last.

'So, that's why you've gone so pale? You thought somebody'd stolen it? Well, you can relax. It's quite safe.' He reached under the cane table, drew out her bag, and held it up for her to see. 'I put it out of the way. I thought it would be safer.'

'Thanks. I see.'

Still, Harriet had not moved. Her limbs felt stiff and unsteady with fear. Had he looked inside? Had he seen the ankh?

But as he said nothing, but simply continued to look back at her, a lightly amused, unreadable expression on his face, she told herself to relax. Her secret was safe.

But then he spoke, sending her blood pressure rocketing up again.

'From the look on your face when you thought it had gone missing, anyone would think you had the Crown jewels in there.'

Harriet's stomach did a loop the loop inside her. It took all of her will-power to stop herself from falling to the floor.

Then she forced herself to smile. It had been an innocent joke. He had no idea how close he was to the truth!

'You know how we women are about our bags,' she answered, dropping her weight from her sagging legs on to the sunbed. 'Without our bags, we'd be totally lost.'

'Well, yours is quite safe.' He handed it across to her. Then, as though he had no more interest in the subject, he lay back on his sunbed and closed his eyes.

Harriet, too, stretched herself out, struggling to compose herself, forcing herself to loosen her nervous grip on her bag and return it to where he had placed it under the cane table.

But just as she was starting to recover from her fright, Dexter proceeded to deliver a far more lethal shock.

In a tone as calm as the surface of the swimming-pool, without raising his head, without even glancing across at her, he said, 'Oh, by the way... Since you're feeling so much better, I've made another appointment for you with the director of the museum. For tomorrow afternoon at five o'clock...'

He paused just an instant before driving home the final thrust. 'But you won't be going alone. I'll be coming with you.'

CHAPTER SEVEN

HARRIET froze like a statue, her heart thundering inside her. She stared in horror at the figure on the sunbed. 'That really won't be necessary,' she stuttered incoherently.

Dexter half turned then to glance at her. 'Oh, but I insist,' he told her. 'The museum director is a very good friend of mine. It will be my pleasure to accompany you.'

She ought to have guessed that, Harriet thought now, belatedly. Anyone of any importance would be on Dexter's list of contacts. That was probably how he had found out about the appointment she'd had for yesterday.

But such details, for the moment, were neither here nor there. All that mattered was that she find a way to wriggle out of tomorrow's appointment.

Clearing her throat, forcing her voice to sound normal, she told him, 'It won't be necessary for me to meet the director, so I'd be grateful if you'd just cancel the appointment.'

'Cancel it? Why? I thought you wanted to see him?' Dexter's tone was a masterpiece of innocent incomprehension.

'I've changed my mind. It won't be necessary.' He suspected something. That was perfectly obvious. She found it hard to look at him as she continued, 'It was silly of me to make the appointment in the first place.'

'I must say it made me curious.' He smiled calmly across at her. 'By a complete coincidence I had to phone the museum yesterday and spoke to the same chap you'd spoken with earlier. When he told me my assistant had made an appointment to meet the director I confess I was just a little surprised.'

Then he added, before she could say anything in response, 'I suppose you're wondering how he came to know you were my assistant? That's easily answered. I'm pretty well-known here, and enough people have heard your name and seen us together for the word to get around.'

In fact, that was the last thing Harriet had been wondering. What she'd been wondering was how she was going to talk herself out of this mess!

She struggled to keep her head clear and control her panic—which wasn't easy with Dexter watching her with those piercing black eyes of his. He hadn't said another word, but he was waiting for an explanation.

A lie, she knew, was the only thing that could save her. It went against the grain, but she had no choice.

She took a deep breath. 'It was nothing important... The reason I arranged to meet him, I mean. I just wanted to know more about the history of Luxor and Egypt... I thought he was probably the best person to speak to...'

As lies went, she had to confess, it was pretty feeble and transparent. But then lying was a pursuit at which Harriet had never excelled.

Dexter frowned across at her from his sunbed. He said, 'You could have spoken to me.'

'I suppose I could. It was silly of me, really. We were passing the museum one day and I just suddenly thought of it...'

'I see. It was just an impulse?'

'Just a silly impulse.'

The trouble with lies, she thought forlornly, was that one never proved to be enough. You had to keep spinning more and more in order to back up the first one, until you were entangled in an ever-growing web of deceit. She gazed at the ground, wishing she could sink into it.

Dexter's eyes were on her. 'I thought there might have been some reason, some specific reason, why you wanted to speak to the director in private...'

He let the observation hang for a moment between them, and Harriet could feel her heart pressing like a clenched fist against her ribs. He wasn't going to let her off. He hadn't swallowed her excuses. He was going to torture her until she spilled out the truth.

She swallowed. 'No, I can assure you there wasn't.'

There was another short pause, then Dexter shrugged and surprised her. 'In that case... Since there was no specific reason... I'll cancel tomorrow's appointment, if that's what you wish.'

'Yes, I think that's best.' She forced herself to look at him, scarcely able to believe he had actually let her off the hook. 'There's really no point in going ahead with it.'

'Consider it done, then.' He reached for his beer, took a long, slow mouthful, and leaned back more comfortably. Then he slanted her a look. 'And remember,' he told her, 'if there's anything you want to know about the history of Luxor and Egypt...all you have to do is ask me.'

He paused and smiled at her. 'I'm at your service.'

The subject of the museum was not mentioned again, much to Harriet's heartfelt relief. Though she realised that now she was faced with a dilemma: where was she to get the advice she needed on what to do with the ankh?

I shall just have to wait until we're due to leave Luxor, she decided, then simply hand over the ankh to the museum director and let him do with it whatever needs to be done.

There would be no keeping this final gesture from Dexter and no way of avoiding his inevitable wrath. But at least by then her job would be done and he would have no choice, however angry he was with her, but to hand over the money he had agreed to pay her—and then they need never set eyes on one another again.

That was a pleasing thought, but there was one remaining worry. How was she to get the ankh safely back into her safe box when Dexter, in his current guise as guardian angel, rarely left her side for more than a minute?

It was a little after seven, just as the sun was sinking, a fiery orange ball hovering over the horizon, when Dexter suggested, 'How would you fancy going to the Karnak Temple show this evening? It starts at eight. If we hurry we could make it. Then we could have dinner together afterwards.'

Harriet felt her eyebrows soar. What's the matter? she almost asked him. Aren't you seeing Nabila tonight?

But she bit back the comment. It was none of her business—and why would she wish to make such a petty comment anyway? It would have sounded like a reproach, as though she were accusing him of having neglected her. And the very idea of such a thing was utterly ludicrous. She was delighted that he kept out of her way in the evenings!

So, stifling her astonishment, she smiled and replied, 'That's a lovely idea. I'd like that very much.'

'Then we'd better get our skates on.' Dexter rose from his sunbed and proceeded to pull on his shorts and T-shirt. 'We ought to aim to be on our way by a quarter to eight at the latest.'

Up in her room, Harriet showered quickly, blew her hair dry, and rummaged through her wardrobe. What to wear? Her fingers hovered uncertainly. This would be her first evening out since her arrival in Luxor and she felt foolishly excited at the prospect.

But as she pulled out the most glamorous outfit she'd brought with her—a pretty silk two-piece in her favourite shade of blue—she suddenly caught the eye of her reflection in the mirror.

Was she out of her mind? She was treating this like a date! And this was definitely no date. Perish the thought! All this was was an evening out with her boss. There was no need for all this silly excitement. In fact, it was totally out of place.

Impatiently she pushed the hanger back on the rail. A simple blouse and cotton skirt would fit the bill perfectly. A smart but unexceptional outfit for what would probably be a pleasant but unexceptional evening.

When Harriet stepped into the lobby, Dexter was waiting for her by the fountain, dressed in a pair of immaculate white trousers and an equally immaculate fine silk shirt.

The blue outfit she had rejected might have done him more justice, Harriet found herself reflecting as she walked towards him. For he did, even more than usual, look quite heart-stoppingly stunning.

Though she reminded herself quickly that it was not her job to do him justice. That was Nabila's role, not hers!

He was rising to his feet, smiling. 'Good. You're early. It's nice to meet a woman who's so habitually punctual.'

For some silly reason his quick, easy smile and teasing, humourous tone had caused Harriet's heart to tighten. She squashed the feeling as she smiled back at him and answered, 'And I, too, appreciate a man who doesn't keep me waiting.'

'So, we are capable, after all, of pleasing one another.' As he said it, he deliberately held her gaze. 'Even if only in such relatively trifling matters...'

It was a reference to one of their early exchanges, when Dexter had observed, in typically cutting fashion, that neither of them was ever likely to please the other.

Only now there had been no sharp edge to his voice, and the dark eyes were filled with warm, gentle irony. He *has* changed, Harriet decided, for once making no effort to reject the answering warm flicker inside her. His feelings towards me are no longer wholly negative. If nothing else, that boded well for the evening ahead!

A couple of minutes later they were on their way, their taxi heading for the other end of the city, where the ancient Karnak Temple lay. As she peered out through the window, Harriet felt a thrill of excitement. She had read about the Sound and Light show. Now she was actually going to experience it!

'Stick with me.'

Dexter caught her by the arm as they climbed out of the taxi and headed towards the massive temple, along an avenue lined on either side with ram-headed sphinxes, to join the crowd that was already gathering, abuzz with expectation.

'Let's try to make sure we don't lose one another,' he added.

The way he was holding on to her arm there was little fear of that, Harriet reflected to herself with wry amusement. He evidently didn't relish the prospect of their being separated and his having to search for her among all these people!

He remained glued to her side throughout the spectacle that followed, as the lights switched on and the show began. And what unfolded was, for Harriet, pure enchantment.

It was magical to be standing there in that two-thousand-year-old temple with its massive carved columns reaching up to the sky while the search-lights shifted from one spot to another, now lighting up the gigantic statue of the Colossus, now shifting to a row of pharaohs carved from stone.

And all the while a voice that seemed to come from the heavens recited the history of this ancient, once-sacred place, built in honour of the great god

Amon. The atmosphere was electric. Harriet could feel shivers down her spine.

'See the obelisk over there?' Suddenly Dexter bent to whisper. 'It was built for her king by Queen Hatshepsut. She originally wanted to have it made of solid gold, but when that proved impossible—there just wasn't enough gold around!—she decided to have it carved from marble instead.'

Harriet glanced at the slender obelisk that rose thirty metres into the sky. 'How incredible,' she answered. 'What a romantic story!'

'The whole thing is carved from one solid piece of marble. It took seven months to bring the marble here from the quarries of Aswan.'

Harriet shook her head. As a token of love, Queen Hatshepsut's obelisk was in a realm of its own! And here it still stood, two millenniums later, for all the world to see and gasp at in wonder.

And just for a moment she envied the long-dead queen. To have shared a love worthy of such a monument was something most women could only dream of.

She sighed. 'She must have loved her king very much.'

'Apparently she did. And she wanted all the world to know it.'

'Quite right. That's the way it ought to be when you're in love.'

'You reckon?' He turned and smiled at her. His tone was teasing. Then he surprised her by nodding. 'I tend to agree.'

Harriet was grateful for the darkness, for a blush touched her cheeks. It was something about the way he was looking down at her, something about the way they were standing so close together and the intimate way his arm was linked with hers.

No, it was none of these things, she told herself hurriedly, glancing away, turning back to the spectacle. It was simply a friendly feeling of pleasure that they should actually agree about something for once.

But that didn't quite explain why her eyes drifted back to him to fix for a moment on the pharaoh-like profile, nor why the thought suddenly occurred to her that this past week and a half in Luxor had undoubtedly been the most memorable time of her entire life.

'Come on.'

After the first half of the show was over, Dexter led her through the crowd to take their places in the front row of the bank of tiered seats that overlooked the sacred lake.

Smiling, he bent to tell her, 'You're really going to like this bit. This bit's even more spectacular than what you've just seen.'

And it was. As light flashed and strobed across the sky, the very heavens the vast backdrop for the dazzling display that unfolded, Harriet glanced across to him. 'You weren't kidding. This is the most incredible thing I've ever seen!'

'I knew you'd like it.' He caught her eye and winked at her. 'That was why I brought you. I wanted to see that look of yours... When you look just like a child at Christmas.'

Harriet giggled. There had been absolutely no malice in the remark. She turned to look at him. 'I hope you don't mind my saying so, but you look a bit like a kid at Christmas yourself!'

'Do I?' He squeezed her arm. 'That doesn't surprise me. I reckon I feel a bit like a kid at Christmas.'

Harriet wanted to make a joke of it, to say something flippant, but suddenly she felt transfixed by those deep dark eyes of his. They seemed to be telling her—or did she imagine this?—that the way he was feeling had something to do with her.

Of course she was imagining it. Who was she kidding? Harriet swallowed hard and tore her gaze from his. 'It was really very good of you to take the trouble to bring me. After all, you must have seen this countless times before.'

There was a sudden stiffness in her tone, the stiffness of self-horror. For all at once it had occurred to her that her own current state of pleasure was not entirely unrelated to him. There was no one in the world she would rather have shared this evening with.

Surely not! Again she checked herself. She was certainly glad she'd had someone to share it with. Such an extraordinary experience needed to be shared. And Dexter, indubitably, was the perfect companion—for the simple reason that he was so knowledgeable about it all!

But all the same her flesh tingled as he bent to tell her, 'You're right, I have seen it countless times before, but I've never enjoyed it more than I have tonight.'

At last, too soon, the spectacle was over and the audience began heading for the exit, moving unhurriedly between the statues and the pillars, talking quietly among themselves, reluctant to leave.

Harriet felt the same reluctance to be gone. She paused for a moment beside a row of illuminated stone tablets, elaborately engraved with hieroglyphics.

'I wonder what they say?' she murmured half to herself. 'I wonder if anyone really knows?'

Dexter was standing beside her. 'Oh, we understand them now,' he told her. 'Though you're right, they kept their secrets for thousands of years.'

Then he paused and seemed to hold her eyes for a moment. 'But it is the nature of all secrets to be uncovered in the end.' He continued to hold her eyes. 'Wouldn't you agree?'

What a mysterious remark. Harriet frowned in response. Then he smiled a strange smile. 'Oh, by the way... You forgot this.'

He was holding out her bag to her, still smiling that strange smile. Harriet stared at it as though it were a gun he was pointing at her. She felt the colour leave her cheeks and her limbs grow very still.

'You were obviously distracted.' He handed the bag to her. 'It's just as well I noticed...considering how lost you'd be without it.'

Trying to conceal her shaking hands, Harriet took the bag from him. 'Thank you,' she muttered, scarcely daring to look at him. How could she have been so stupid? she chastised herself in horror. The bag could have been stolen, and the precious ankh with it!

And suddenly her mind was filled with Dexter's observation about secrets and how they were always destined to be uncovered. Had he been trying to tell her something? Did he know more than he was saying? Did he know about her secret, the ankh?

As they headed for the street she dismissed that idea. If he knew, he would not be behaving so civilly, and neither would he be keeping the knowledge to himself. He would long ago have confiscated the ankh—and torn her into shreds into the bargain. And a quick check had reassured her that the ankh was still in her bag.

Out in the street the crowd was dispersing, some climbing into the waiting *calèches* and taxis, others setting off to make the journey home on foot.

Dexter turned to Harriet suddenly. 'How hungry are you?' he demanded. 'How quickly do you want to get back to the hotel?'

There was a smile in his eyes that made her smile back curiously. 'I'm not particularly hungry, but why do you ask?'

'If you're not in a hurry, we can take a *calèche.*' He took her by the arm and led across the square to where a line of the horse-drawn carriages was waiting. 'We can go the long way home and have a moonlight tour of Luxor.'

'What a splendid idea!' Harriet beamed with pleasure. The perfect ending, she was thinking, to what had been a wonderful evening. An evening that had turned out to be anything but unexceptional!

A moment later Dexter was helping her up into the carriage behind the driver and they were settling back against the red leather seats. Then, at a crack of the whip, they were setting off, the horse moving at an easy, comfortable trot, the brass bells jangling, hooves clacking against the cobble-stones.

'I told the driver we're in no hurry. But if you start to feel hungry, just let me know and I can ask him to speed things up.'

'Oh, don't do that! This is wonderful! Tell him to take as long as he can!'

And so they set off on a leisurely tour of Luxor, clopping round deserted back streets, winding in and out of alleyways, seeing sights that most tourists never saw.

'See that mosque? It's one of the oldest in the city.' As they trotted along, Dexter pointed things out to her. 'This is a new school, just recently completed. And round the back there is where you'll find the old bazaar.'

'Is that where you bought your carpet?' Harriet smiled as she said it. She was thoroughly enjoying this sightseeing tour. And she was enjoying, too, listening to Dexter talk about the city. He knew so much about it. He made it come alive.

'Yes, that's where I bought it. In a little shop a couple of streets away.' He met her eyes and smiled back at her. 'I can take you there some time.'

As he had spoken, the carriage had jolted on an uneven cobble-stone, and just for an instant Harriet's thigh had brushed Dexter's. The effect was like an electric shock to her senses.

She pulled away instantly, aware that her heart was racing. 'No, I don't think so. I'm not like you. I don't have money to spend on carpets.'

The words had come out sounding far more prickly than she'd intended. They'd been a reflex action. A bid for self-protection. Though what she could possibly need protecting from she couldn't imagine.

As a silence fell between them, she felt a spasm of irritation. That prickly response of hers had been quite unnecessary. And she'd been enjoying herself so much that she hated to spoil the mood. She wanted things to continue the way they'd been before her little outburst.

She glanced up at the sky, as though seeking inspiration. Then her eyes widened and she pointed. 'Oh, look! It's a new moon!'

'So it is.' Dexter followed her pointing finger. Then he told her, 'They have a special name for the new moon in these parts.'

He had forgiven her her outburst, Harriet thought with some relief. His tone was unchanged, still warm and light-hearted.

She swivelled round to look at him. 'What name?' she asked him curiously. But, as she looked into his face, she had to turn away again to disguise the sudden hectic clamour in her heart.

Those black eyes of his had seemed to graze against her. She thought she saw a message there that made her blood burn.

Feeling foolish, Harriet clutched the side of the calèche, as though it were a lifebelt keeping her safe from danger.

What danger? The question repeated itself in her head. Was she going crazy or something?

Well, if she wasn't, she was certainly behaving as though she were! Deliberately, Harriet released her grip on the side of the calèche and turned with forced composure as Dexter answered her question.

'In these parts they call the new moon the Prophet's eyebrow. I've always thought it was rather a lovely name.'

Harriet was still struggling for equilibrium. She frowned a little. 'What does that mean? The Prophet's eyebrow?'

'It's a reference to the Prophet Mohamed.' Harriet followed his gaze, as he glanced up at the sky and the moon again. 'And if you think about it, it's a very apt description. That thin silver crescent looks just like the eyebrow of an old man.'

He was right. It did. Harriet relaxed and smiled with pleasure. 'The Prophet's eyebrow! That's a wonderful name. Every time I see a new moon I shall remember that.'

It was at that precise moment, just as she was relaxing in her seat again, that one wheel of the *calèche* struck another loose cobble-stone. The carriage gave a jolt, throwing Harriet sideways, and suddenly, before she could do anything to stop herself, she was falling against Dexter, one hand on his chest, her body colliding with his, pressing against him.

That was sheer chance, but what happened next was not.

Instead of pulling away instantly, as she had fully intended doing, Harriet found herself hesitating for just a fraction of a second. A fatal fraction of a second, she would tell herself later. Although, even at the time, she had known what it would lead to.

'Are you all right?' Dexter was glancing down at her, his face so close to hers that his chin was brushing her hair.

Harriet nodded soundlessly. But still she did not move. And then, as the second passed, it was too late to think of moving.

She felt his arm slip round her waist and she shivered at the touch of him. A shiver of delight, a shiver of sheer pleasure. Then his fingers were in her hair, making her scalp burn, and his eyes, like molten velvet, were pouring into hers, making her head swim, taking the breath from her body.

Beneath the hand that was pressed against his chest she could feel the strong, swift beat of his heart. Perhaps, she wondered with a shiver of excitement, he could feel hers beating, too.

But that was all she had time to think. Suddenly he was bending towards her. Suddenly, warm and soft, his lips were closing over hers.

It was a kiss that Harriet would remember for ever. She had never been kissed like this before.

Never had the touch of any man's lips started such a fire in her. She had never felt the blood pound so fiercely in her veins. And she had never before experienced such an exquisite sense of pleasure. The intensity of it left her breathless and gasping for more.

He was pushing back her hair, kissing her temple, her hair-line, triggering darts of excitement up and down her spine. 'We'll spend tomorrow together, at leisure,' he was saying. 'Just you and me. How does that sound?'

It sounded like heaven. Harriet sighed and leaned against him. 'Yes,' she agreed. 'I'd like that very much.'

He kissed her lips again and held her against him. 'I reckon it'll do us good to get to know each other better. Share a few secrets. That sort of thing.'

Harriet smiled. Suddenly the thought of getting to know him better made her stomach turn happy somersaults inside her. She pressed her open palm against his hard chest, loving the warm, virile, muscular feel of him.

'Yes, I'd like that,' she answered in a whisper.

'Then that's what we'll do.' He caressed her cheek softly. 'I'm sure we've got lots of things to discover about each other. Perhaps things we ought to have revealed to one another long ago.'

Harriet leaned against him and nodded silently. Suddenly she wanted to know everything about this man. Every tiny detail. To know him inside out.

'That's settled, then.' As the *calèche* emerged from the back streets out on to the busy Corniche, Dexter drew back a little, but remained with his arm around her, allowing her to settle comfortably against him.

Then suddenly he added, as thought it were an afterthought, 'I'll have to leave you to your own devices in the evening, however. I'm afraid I have a prior engagement.'

The words, spoken so casually, were like a douse of cold water. Briefly, Harriet had forgotten about Nabila, the beautiful dark-haired girlfriend with whom he always spent his evenings.

She felt a coldness rush through her. What had she been thinking of? How could she have allowed him, when she knew he belonged to another, to kiss her and caress her and hold her that way? Did she have no shame? Did she wish to be his plaything?

Before she could speak, they were approaching the hotel. The *calèche* came to a halt and in turn they climbed down. And suddenly Harriet knew what she must do.

She stood to one side and waited as Dexter paid the driver. Then, as he approached her and they began the short walk to the main door, she looked up at him and spoke as calmly as she was able.

'I've been thinking, and I've decided your plan for tomorrow isn't such a good idea, after all. I think we should keep our relationship strictly business. And since I'm feeling fine now, I suggest we just get back to work tomorrow.'

'I see. That was a sudden change of mind.' He had stopped to look down at her. 'Any particular reason?'

Harriet looked him in the eye. 'My reasons are personal. I really don't think I'm obliged to explain them.' She felt angry with him suddenly for having misled her, for having encouraged her to mislead herself. Why should she offer him explanations when he ought to be aware of the reasons himself?

With a toss of her head, she turned and headed for the door.

But that was when he caught her arm, stopping her in her tracks. 'Not so fast, young lady.' His eyes had grown flinty. 'Since that's the way you want things, I'm afraid I have one small demand.'

Harriet glared at him in fury. How dared he lay a hand on her? Who the devil did he think he was? 'What kind of demand?'

'This.'

Before she realised what was happening, he had snatched her bag from her and was reaching inside it. He drew out the package of tissues that contained the gold ankh. 'I'd feel happier if this were in my safe box.'

Then, as Harriet stood there transfixed, her bones turned to water, he thrust the bag back at her and turned sharply on his heel. He paused only for a second, before disappearing through the hotel doors, to warn her over his shoulder, 'We'll discuss this more thoroughly in the morning.'

CHAPTER EIGHT

HARRIET stood rooted to the spot as Dexter swept through the hotel doors. I'm done for, she was thinking. This is the end. Now he'll have my guts for garters.

At last, on stiff limbs, she headed for the lobby and took the lift up to her room. She lay down on the bed and stared, blank-eyed, at the ceiling. He must have discovered the ankh earlier, when she'd left her bag behind at the temple. He must have looked inside. Or maybe it had fallen out. Either way, her moment of distraction had proved fatal.

He'll tear me apart, she thought, remembering his last words to her: 'We'll discuss this more thoroughly in the morning.' Tomorrow promised to be a day she would not easily forget.

Harriet closed her eyes as a worm of shame writhed within her. Neither would she easily forget what had happened tonight.

What had got into her? she asked herself now in misery. On the *calèche* ride from Karnak Temple she had behaved like a wanton, virtually inviting him to kiss her. He hadn't needed much persuasion—what man ever did?—but the signals she'd been sending had been loud and clear anyway.

And it hadn't been just a fleeting moment of flirtation. She had wanted him, desperately, with an intensity beyond fighting. In that fraction of a second, when she'd been thrown against him and had suddenly looked up into his eyes, she'd been consumed by a helpless, irresistible yearning to fall into his arms and feel his lips against hers.

It was shocking. She knew that. But she could not deny it.

It was the effect of that magical light show, she told herself. It was the moon. It was that romantic ride in the *calèche*. It was that silly, charming tale about the Prophet's eyebrow. It was the fact that she'd been feeling relaxed and happy. Somehow, all these things had got mixed up in her brain and she had ended up projecting them on to Dexter Ross.

She sighed, finding some comfort in this rationalisation. Dexter himself had really had nothing to do with it. She would have reacted just the same with any other attractive man. It was a moment of madness. It had meant nothing whatsoever. Something had simply short-circuited in her brain.

But that was a fantasy and she knew it. She remembered the dark eyes and how they had poured into her. Like molten black velvet, playing havoc with her senses. No man she had ever known had eyes like Dexter, eyes that could reach down to touch her very soul. Eyes whose sinful powers she had no power to resist.

But such thoughts were far too disturbing to dwell on. Harriet pushed them from her as she got ready for bed and tried to concentrate instead on tomorrow's confrontation and what tactics she should use to defend herself.

For any sane person in Harriet's position, that would have qualified, without question, as the most urgent preoccupation—how to contain the storm she knew he was about to unleash on her.

But when at last she fell asleep, what was still uppermost in Harriet's mind, in spite of all her desperate efforts to banish it, was the memory of those shameful, blissful moments in the *calèche*.

'I suggest we have breakfast—separately—then meet in the sitting-room for a chat.'

Dexter's call woke Harriet just after seven, and he sounded every bit as grim as she'd expected.

'Be there at eight-thirty sharp,' he commanded brusquely, then hung up before she had time to reply.

Harriet rose wearily from her bed. She had slept briefly and badly. She was really in no fit state for a fight. Which was not to say, she rebuked herself sharply, as she stretched and headed for the bathroom to take a shower, that she had any intention of letting him trample all over her. She'd had a perfectly honourable reason for what she'd done. And she would let him know that in no uncertain fashion!

She had breakfast on her bedroom balcony overlooking the Nile, wondering with a twist of sadness as she watched the boats on the river if this was destined to be the last breakfast she would ever have here. It seemed logical to suppose that, once Dexter had finished yelling at her, his next move would be to pack her off on the first plane back to England.

How terribly sad. She frowned at the prospect. She had fallen a little in love with this place.

It was eight-thirty precisely when, dressed in white trousers and a pink shirt, Harriet stepped through the door that led to the sitting-room. She was still feeling nervous, but she was ready to stand up to him. If she must go, she had decided, it would be with a bang, not a whimper!

He was standing by the window that overlooked the balcony, a tall, daunting figure in sand trousers and white shirt. He had his back to her. He did not turn round.

'Close the door,' he said, 'and kindly take a seat.'

Harriet closed the door, but remained standing where she was. His tone had been the tone one might use to command a dog.

Cuttingly, she shot back at him, 'While you're issuing orders...do you have any particular preference as to which seat I take?'

Dexter turned then to look at her, the dark eyes narrowed. 'I'm surprised. I had expected at least a show of humility. One in your position has little cause for defiance.'

So, he had expected her to come in grovelling and repentant. Harriet felt a dart of triumph that she had so resoundingly disappointed him.

She said, 'I see no cause for humility. I'm not in any way ashamed of what I did.'

'That is self-evident.' His eyes swept her with a harsh look that was touched, Harriet thought fleetingly, with a shadow of regret. As though he believed that she'd somehow let him down.

For an instant, in response, she felt almost sorry herself. But she shook that feeling from her as he continued, 'It would appear that you take pride in theft and dishonesty?'

'Theft and dishonesty?' Harriet blinked across at him. For though the second part was true—she *had* been dishonest—his accusation of stealing was way off the mark! 'You're wrong,' she assured him. 'I'm not a thief.'

'No?' He laughed at that, as he moved away from the window, and came to stand, a few feet away from her, in the middle of the room. 'You may not like the sound of the label, my dear Harriet, but a person who takes objects which do not belong to them is, in common parlance, known as a thief.'

Harriet looked into his face. Was he bluffing, she wondered, or did he really believe that she was a thief? Oddly, that possibility had never occurred to her. She'd assumed he would guess why she'd taken the ankh—purely and simply to keep it from him.

She was still wondering as he demanded, 'Why did you do it? Wasn't the money I was paying you enough to pay your builders' bills? Or were you simply motivated by greed?'

'No, I wasn't motivated by greed. I——'

'Did you plan to smuggle the ankh back to London, then find some collector who would pay you a good price?' He cut across her, the dark eyes ablaze with furious anger. 'Do you know what the penalties are for trying to smuggle these things out of Egypt? How do you fancy spending some time in an Egyptian jail?'

Harriet was suddenly wishing that she'd sat down, after all. If he was bluffing, he was making a very good job of it. Her legs, all at once, felt distinctly shaky.

'You're talking nonsense!' She tried to keep her voice steady. 'You know as well as I do that I wasn't trying to steal it!'

'Do I? And how am I likely to know that? The evidence, if you will permit, points entirely the other way.'

'I know that, but——'

'But nothing! And I have a witness. When you so inconveniently collapsed in a faint in the strong-room, I wasn't the only one who saw the pendant fall from your hand. The young man from Reception saw it all as clearly as I did.'

Harriet's cheeks had grown pale. What was he saying? That she had not, after all, slipped the ankh back in her bag? That he had known as long ago as that that she was hiding it?

For a moment she was speechless. Totally bewildered. 'So, why,' she asked at last, 'did you put the ankh back in my bag?'

Dexter raised one black eyebrow. 'Perhaps I'm wondering that myself now.' He turned away abruptly and paced the floor for a moment. 'I'm beginning to think that was a mistake on my part.'

'Perhaps it was to cover your own tracks.' Suddenly, a thought had occurred to Harriet. She squared the shoulders that had sagged a little earlier. 'Perhaps you pretended to the receptionist that the ankh wasn't valuable, just something I'd picked up in the bazaar. Perhaps you put it back in my bag to give yourself time to work out a way of getting your hands on it yourself!'

Dexter paused in his pacing. 'And why would I want to do that?'

'So that you could add it to your precious collection!' Harriet straightened and glared at him. 'That's why I took it—as I'm sure you're already quite well aware! To stop you taking it for yourself!'

'Oh, I'm sure to believe that!' Dexter was scornful. 'I'm sure to believe your motives were the highest!' He swung round on her. 'You took it because you knew it was valuable. Because you needed it to make up the money your ex-fiancé stole from you! Your ex-fiancé,' he added disparagingly, 'whose memory still causes you such pain!'

She had been about to deny that last part, but changed her mind. It was irrelevant. Instead, she repeated, 'I didn't take the ankh for the reason you're suggesting,' she repeated. 'I took it in order to save it from you!'

But he was scarcely listening to her. He cut in roughly, 'Unfortunately, you weren't sure just how much it was worth ... Hence the appointment with the museum director. No doubt you intended to be very discreet. No doubt you would have kept your enquiries strictly hypothetical. If one were to stumble upon an ancient Egyptian ankh, how much would it be worth? That would have been your line of questioning.'

'You're totally wrong!' Harriet stepped towards him in anger. 'All I wanted to ask him was what I ought to do with it! All I wanted was to find out how to keep it safe from you!'

'I'll bet!' With an eloquent gesture Dexter waved aside her argument. Then he shook his head. 'You know, I was prepared to give you a chance. That was why I said nothing, why I put it back in your bag. In order to give you a chance to own up to what you'd done. I thought your conscience might finally get the better of you.'

'I see. You were hoping I would hand it over to you. That would have been really convenient, wouldn't it?'

He ignored her accusation. 'Of course, it was a risk. Knowing you were carrying that thing around in your bag meant I had to keep a constant eye on you. Partly in case you lost it—which you very nearly did—and partly in case you decided to find a buyer here. It meant I had to stick with you every single minute.'

Harriet felt herself recoil. His words had pierced her like hot needles. She had allowed herself to believe that he had been acting out of concern for her, that he had even, just a little, come to enjoy being with her. And she had allowed herself to feel flattered and pleased by that belief.

He proceeded to pierce her even more deeply.

'Right up until the end I was prepared to give you a chance. Yesterday evening, when I proposed that we spend the day together, I was hoping that a bit of time spent quietly in one another's company might encourage you finally to come clean. I didn't want to have to be forced to report you to the authorities.'

That final veiled threat, though she knew it ought to be the reason, was not what had caused Harriet's heart to stand still. Suddenly she remembered how, as they had sat together in the *calèche*, she leaning happily against him, he with his arm around her, he had spoken of how they would spend the day together.

What was it he'd said? Something about sharing secrets? 'I'm sure we've got lots of things to discover about each another. Perhaps things we ought to have revealed to one another long ago.'

She blushed now for shame. How naïve she had been. She had believed—and the belief had been like a light flooding through her—that what he'd wanted was for the two of them to get to know each other better. And all he'd really been interested in was the ankh.

As she sought to smother the memory, she was barely aware of what he was saying. She just stood there, appalled at herself and sick to her soul.

But she caught the final sentence. 'So I've decided against that. I've decided not to report to the authorities. After all, the ankh's safe now. And that's what matters most.'

'Safe for you to find some way to add to your collection!' Harriet glared at him, hating him for having misled her, but hating herself more for having been so easily misled. 'But don't think you'll get away with it! Don't think you can smuggle it out! I intend to inform the director of Luxor museum that I found it and that you took it from me!'

'I've no intention of smuggling it out.' He regarded her calmly. 'As I've already told you, that sort of thing's illegal.'

He was right, of course. He was too sophisticated to go in for smuggling. He would find some other, legal, if no less devious, way to misappropriate it. He was an expert, after all. He did it all the time.

'Besides,' he added, as she continued to glare impotently at him, 'the museum director has already been apprised of its existence. So there's really no need for you to trouble yourself on that score.'

He paused. 'The only score on which you need trouble yourself now are the arrangements for your earliest return to England. I can scarcely continue to work alongside a thief.'

Harriet shook her head in vain. 'You're wrong. I'm not a thief.'

'I shall accompany you this afternoon to organise your ticket.' He glanced at his watch. 'This morning I have things to do.'

Harriet could guess what at least one of those things would be. 'I suppose you'll be contacting my stand-in,' she observed drily, trying to ignore the plummet of disappointment inside her. She had known he would send her back, but she'd been hoping that he might not.

'I suppose I shall.' He delivered her a harsh look. 'Let's hope she proves to be a little more reliable than you.'

Harriet was suddenly beyond protesting. He would never believe her. And, even if he did, what difference would it make? She might succeed in persuading him that she was not a thief, but there still remained the fact that she had acted against him. And that he would never be able to forgive.

He was turning away, but he paused now to inform her, 'Before you leave, I shall of course pay you for the work you have already done. Then we can finally close the books on this unhappy association.'

A moment later he was turning and heading for the door, leaving Harriet still standing in the middle of the room, aware that the sense of total desolation she was feeling was grossly out of proportion with the calamity that had befallen her.

She had lost her temporary job and a bit of much-need money. That, in the end, was all it boiled down to.

So why did she suddenly feel as though a terrible darkness had descended, locking her heart in wretchedness, as though in a tomb? Why did she suddenly feel as though she would never see light again?

Harriet spent the remainder of the morning at her word processor, transcribing the last of Dexter's tapes. Keeping busy was preferable to sitting around idly. Keeping busy helped to shake off her sense of despair.

But though by lunchtime she was feeling a great deal better, almost resigned to her imminent departure from Luxor, there was still something in the back of her mind that bothered her.

Dexter's claim that he believed she had meant to steal the ankh had sounded so convincing that in the end she had believed it. He'd refused to consider, even for a moment, that she had taken it in order to save it from him. And there was just something about that fact that troubled her.

Yet there was no reason why it should, she told herself impatiently. He had refused to consider that she might have acted out of decency simply because he had no decency himself. He just assumed that everyone else was as grasping as he was.

Harriet had lunch—her last, she thought sadly—down by the pool, and was deeply relieved when Dexter failed to show. From now until she climbed

aboard her plane, the less they had to do with one
another the better.

Yet she would miss him, she found herself reflecting as the waiter brought her coffee and she
stared down emptily into its blackness. She suspected he would not be easy to forget.

She shook herself inwardly. What a foolish
thought! She would expunge him from her mind
the minute she turned her back on him! What would
remain with her was not the memory of the man,
but the magical new world he had revealed to her.
For, insufferable as he was, he had taught her a lot.

It was late afternoon before the summons came.
Harriet was down by the pool, enjoying a final
swim, when one of the hotel staff came to tell her,
'Miss Kaye, I have a message from Mr Ross. He
says he'll meet you in the lobby in an hour's time.'

'Thank you.' Harriet forced herself to smile pol-
itely. But her face felt stiff. She felt shocked and
distressed by the fierce sense of sadness that had
suddenly gripped her.

This was it. There was to be no stay of execution.
For instinctively she had guessed at the purpose of
the meeting. He was going to take her to the travel
agency to organise her ticket.

She was not mistaken. An hour later she found
him waiting for her by the fountain in the lobby.
And for one foolish moment her heart skipped a
beat, just as it had when she had seen him standing
there last night.

Only last night he had been smiling. Now he was
not.

'The taxi's waiting.' That was the extent of his
greeting. Then, with barely a glance at her, he was

leading her across the lobby and through the automatic doors, out into the hotel forecourt.

'Thomas Cook's,' he told the driver, as they climbed into the cab.

It was only a short drive. They would be there in no time. Harriet felt herself huddle in growing misery. It doesn't matter, she kept telling herself. I don't care. But she did.

They were approaching the Winter Palace when it happened, just a stone's throw from the Thomas Cook office. Suddenly, just ahead of them, a child of eight or nine ran out into the road, straight into the path of another taxi. There was a screech of tyres, then a sickening thump, followed by a moment of total silence before the entire street erupted.

Suddenly, everyone was shouting and yelling at once. People were rushing to the spot where the child had fallen. Suddenly, all around them, reigned confusion and chaos.

Dexter acted instantly. 'Stop!' he told the driver. Then he turned to Harriet. 'You stay where you are.'

Before he had finished the sentence he was jumping out of the cab and running to the spot where the accident had happened. And that was the moment at which the entire scene altered.

Suddenly, out of chaos, there was order. Craning out of the window, Harriet watched in fascination as with perfect ease Dexter proceeded to take charge. The crowd fell back, as though sensing his authority. All eyes turned to watch him, awaiting his command.

He wasted not a moment as he bent over the child, making a quick check to see if it was safe to move him. Then, once he was sure it was, he was scooping the child up, beckoning to the woman who was evidently the child's mother and striding back towards Harriet and the waiting taxi.

He laid the child on the back seat, ushered the weeping mother in beside Harriet, then climbed in beside the driver with a curt command. Then they were speeding along the Corniche, then through a maze of back streets, until at last they came to stop outside a modern new building.

The next half-hour or so was a blur of action, and for Harriet a blur of bafflement and surprise.

As they rushed through the main door—Dexter carrying the child and followed closely by the mother and Harriet—it was instantly obvious that the place was a hospital, and a thoroughly modern and well-equipped one at that.

But what caused Harriet to blink was that the nurse who appeared before them and proceeded to take the child off on a trolley for examination was none other than Nabila, Dexter's girlfriend!

Good grief! she thought. Though it wasn't really surprising. Hadn't she always thought of Nabila as a kind, caring person? It made perfect sense that she should turn out to be a nurse.

But a couple of minutes later, there was another shock in store.

As Harriet and Dexter waited outside the examination room—Nabila had invited the mother to accompany her child inside—along the corridor suddenly appeared another familiar figure. It took a moment for Harriet to recognise him, but then she blinked in surprise again. It was Dr Fahmy, the physician who'd come to visit her at the hotel when she was sick!

He greeted Harriet and Dexter briefly. 'I hear there's been an accident?'

Dexter nodded towards the examination room. 'Yes, Nabila's with the boy now.'

'Then he's in good hands.' Dr Fahmy smiled. Then he stepped towards the examination room. 'I'll just have a quick check.'

A matter of minutes later, he re-emerged—with Nabila and the child and the child's mother at his heels.

'He's fine. A couple of stitches in his leg was all he needed. In a day or two's time he'll be as right as rain.' His words were confirmed by the bright smile on the child's face and the look of relief on that of the mother.

'Does that mean he can go home now?' Dexter was rising to his feet. 'If so, I'll accompany them. The taxi's waiting outside.'

As Dr Fahmy nodded, Nabila turned to the boy's mother and spoke to her in Arabic, relaying Dexter's offer. The woman smiled at him gratefully. '*Shokrun*,' she told him.

But Dexter was shaking his head and lifting the child into his arms, protesting that no thanks were needed. Then he turned to Harriet. 'Do you mind waiting here while I take them home? There's no point in all of us crowding into the taxi. I'll be back for you as quickly as I can.'

'Fine.' As Harriet nodded, Nabila turned to her to say,

'Let's go to the canteen and have a cup of tea.' She glanced at her watch. 'I'm off duty now, and I could do with a bite to eat. I haven't eaten since breakfast.'

That settled, Dexter departed with the mother and child, and Dr Fahmy took his leave. 'I have another patient to see.'

Then Nabila was leading Harriet along the spotless hospital corridors to a big, sunny room tucked away at the back where all ranks of hospital staff, from consultants to porters, sat around the tables, eating and chatting.

Once they'd helped themselves to tea at the self-service counter—tea and a generous prawn salad for Nabila!—the two girls found themselves a quiet table in a corner. As they seated themselves, Nabila observed, 'So, what do you think of Zaynad Hospital?'

Harriet nodded her approval. 'It looks impressive. It's obviously quite new. Have you worked here long?'

'I've worked here since Dexter opened it just over four years ago. And I can assure you it doesn't just look impressive. It's one of the best-equipped hospitals in Egypt.'

Harriet had been about to take a mouthful of her tea, but had paused midway through Nabila's answer.

She blinked in confusion at the dark-haired girl. 'I'm sorry, I think I must have misheard you. I thought you said something about Dexter and the hospital?'

'I said I've worked here ever since Dexter opened it.' Nabila smiled and shook her head. 'Didn't you know? Didn't you know that Zaynad Hospital was Dexter's pet project?'

Harriet had laid down her cup. This was too much to take in. 'This is Dexter's hospital? You mean this place belongs to him?'

'That's exactly what I mean. He built it. He paid for it. He's poured heaven knows how much money into it. And he'll continue to pour money into it. That's guaranteed.' Nabila smiled. 'You see, all the services he offers here are free.'

'You mean Dexter did all this?' Harriet was dumbfounded. 'He never said anything about it to me.'

Nabila laughed. 'That's Dexter for you! He's far too modest. He likes to keep these things to himself.'

As Harriet gaped at her, struggling with this new concept, Nabila continued, 'The hospital is named after Dexter's mother. Her name was Zaynad. Sadly, she died young, at the age of forty-nine. Dexter adored her. He built the hospital in her memory.'

Harriet sat back in her seat. Her brain was spinning. Dexter, a benefactor? It was a hard thought to get to grips with. It was the very opposite of all she'd believed.

'He's planning to build an extension,' Nabila went on to tell her, helping herself to a mouthful of her prawn salad. 'That's why he's been spending so much time here. He's here every evening and most afternoons as well, meeting with architects, overseeing the plans, making arrangements with the builders...'

And seeing you, Harriet thought, as she looked across at Nabila, aware of an uncomfortable sense of envy. For the feeling that Nabila was too good for him had vanished—to be replaced by another notion, alien and bewildering, that any woman would be lucky to have such a man. This new Dexter who was being revealed to her was a man in a million.

It was then, as she dropped her eyes in confusion for a moment, that her gaze suddenly fell on the pretty diamond ring that sparkled on the third finger of Nabila's left hand.

Something jolted inside her. So Nabila was more than just his girlfriend. She was his fiancée. His future wife.

And what difference did that make? Harriet tightened her heart against the sudden plummet of anguish that she felt. Girlfriend or fiancée, it made no difference. All Dexter was to her was her temporary employer. And no longer even that. Her ex-employer.

There was a lull in the conversation as Nabila finished her salad. Then she pushed aside her plate and glanced across at Harriet. 'I understand you made rather an exciting find?' she said. 'Dexter was telling me about it this morning.'

For a moment Harriet failed to understand what she was talking about. Too many inexplicable, disturbing emotions were suddenly swarming around inside her head.

She frowned a little. 'What discovery?' she asked.

Nabila laughed. 'The ankh, of course! Dexter's thrilled. And it was you who found it, I believe?'

Harriet paused to catch her breath. So, he'd told Nabila about the ankh. But from the way the girl was smiling across the table at her, it was clear she hadn't been told the whole messy story!

She nodded. 'Yes, I found it. Quite by accident. I got lost in one of the chambers and there it was.'

'How marvellous!' Nabila was beaming across at her. 'It's so rare these days to find any treasures. No doubt Dexter will be adding it to his collection.'

'No doubt he will.' Harriet felt thrown for a moment. She'd forgotten about this less glowing side of Dexter's character. But now it was a relief to have been reminded.

She added tightly, taking a sip of her tea, 'It's a pretty impressive collection he has.'

'He takes great pains with it.' Nabila sipped her own tea. 'He goes to the most enormous trouble to make sure that each piece is precise in every detail.'

'Precise in every detail?' Harriet frowned across at her. 'What do you mean, "precise in every detail"?'

'Well, copying works of art is an art in itself, and Dexter insists that every copy he has made is a perfect replica of the original. He has a goldsmith in Cairo who does most of the work for him. No doubt his next commission will be to make a copy of the ankh.'

It was gradually dawning on Harriet what Nabila was telling her. She felt her jaw drop as she looked across the table at her. 'You mean that collection of Dexter's . . . all that stuff he has in London . . .? You mean they're all copies? That none of it's original?'

'Of course they're copies!' Nabila giggled. 'The originals are all in museums in Egypt. But it's a passion of Dexter's. Every find he's involved in he likes to have a copy made to keep as a memento.'

'But I thought...'

Harriet stopped herself, feeling suddenly foolish. How could she say what she'd thought? It would sound like a slander!

And it *was* a slander, a shocking slander. Was there anything about this man that she had not totally misjudged?

To hide her bewilderment, she let her eyes drift downwards again, and again caught a glimpse of the diamond on Nabila's finger.

For a moment she fixed on it, a shiver of emotion rushing through her.

Nabila had followed her gaze. 'It's beautiful, isn't it?' There was a smile in her voice. She sounded proud and happy—as indeed, Harriet granted, she'd every right in the world to be.

As Harriet glanced up, agreeing, 'Yes, it is very beautiful,' Nabila added,

'We plan to be married very soon. Just as soon as we can both manage to take time off.'

It was just at that moment, as Harriet's stomach twisted inside her, that Dexter suddenly came striding through the cafeteria door. As Nabila waved to him, smiling happily, Harriet looked into his face and suddenly understood her previous sense of despair.

No wonder I feel so shattered about leaving, she admitted. No wonder I feel as though my life is ending. In spite of all the bad things I once believed of him, I'm totally, hopelessly in love with this man.

CHAPTER NINE

'WHY didn't you tell me?'

They were back at the hotel, sitting out on the balcony, having a drink. On the way back from the clinic, as they'd driven past Thomas Cook's, Dexter had turned to Harriet with a wry smile. 'I think we'll skip the travel arrangements for the moment. I don't know about you, but I've had enough excitement for one day.'

'Me, too.' She'd felt relief and fear collide inside her. Relief that she'd been granted this stay of execution—for after all, above all else, she wanted to stay—and fear at the intensity of the relief that she felt.

Her desire to stay on, she realised now, was not just because of the job, not just because of the money, not just because she had grown attached to Luxor... The reason she wanted to stay was because of Dexter. The thought of leaving him tore her apart.

I've been fooling myself all along, she admitted miserably. I tried to tell myself I hate him. And I believed it. But, in spite of everything, the opposite was true.

She looked across at him now, smothering the misery within her. Did I sense all along that he was not the monster I'd painted him? Was I using him, she wondered, as a scapegoat for Tom—loading Tom's sins on to Dexter and hating him for them?

They were questions there was really no point in asking, for they were questions to which she would never know the answer.

But she could at least demand an answer to the question she had just asked him. 'Why didn't you tell me?' she asked him again.

'Tell you about what?' He cast a guarded look towards her as he took a mouthful of his beer.

'About the hospital, for one thing. Why did you keep it a secret?'

Dexter smiled a slow smile. 'No particular reason. I guess the subject just never came up. I had no idea it would interest you.'

'Of course it interests me!' She said it a little too vehemently. For a moment she wondered if she had revealed herself to him. Her eyes flickered down to the table for a moment, then she raised them again. 'Surely anyone would be interested?'

'Well, you know now, for what it's worth.' Dexter shrugged, then glanced across at her. 'If you'd known before, what difference would it have made?'

'Difference? No difference.' She felt oddly cornered. Had I known, she was thinking, I'd have faced my feelings sooner. I'd have been forced long ago to recognise that I loved you.

But she could scarcely tell him that! She smiled a wry smile and offered a safely watered-down version. 'I'd have realised you're not the monster you seemed to want me to think you were.'

'Did you think I was a monster?' The idea seemed to amuse him. The dark eyebrows lifted. The coal-black eyes danced.

'Something pretty close.' Her heart pressed inside her.

'And why did you think that?'

'Oh, lots of reasons...' She sat back in her seat, struggling for detachment. 'For one thing, all that stuff about your collection of antiquities... You deliberately misled me about that.'

'I never said they were originals.'

'No, but you knew I believed they were. And you knew also that I believed you'd acquired them less than honestly. Why did you let me go on believing that?'

'You're free to believe whatever you wish. And that was evidently what you wished to believe.'

Harriet frowned. Yes, that was true. More or less from the start she'd decided to believe the worst of him. So the fault had indeed been as much hers as his.

And again she thought, I was confusing him with Tom. I was laying at his doorstep all Tom's sins. Right from the start, I didn't give him a chance.

She looked into his face. 'But you could have told me I was wrong.'

'You're right, I suppose I could.' Dexter smiled. 'Perhaps I didn't because I found your indignation appealing. Perhaps I found it something of a novelty to meet someone who cared so passionately about things.'

There was an unexpected intensity of warmth in his tone. Harriet glanced away, overwhelmed by the pleasure that gave her.

She tried to fend off the compliment. 'Is that so rare? Is it so rare for people to feel passionately about things?'

'In my experience, yes.' He regarded her thoughtfully. 'In my experience most people have very little interest in anything outside their own private little sphere.'

Harriet felt a dart of guilt. The shuttered mind-set he was describing was precisely the mind-set she had attributed to him. She had believed he cared nothing for anything outside himself.

And it was so wrong it was almost funny. It was so funny it made her weep.

She glanced down into her orange juice for a moment, then raised her eyes once more to his. 'Tell me something . . . I was wrong, too, wasn't I, about the business of the taxi drivers? You didn't underpay them. In fact, I bet you did the opposite.'

Dexter shook his head and seemed reluctant to answer. 'I agreed on a price that made all of us happy.' And there was something about the way he said it that made Harriet very certain that the price he'd agreed to pay them was not only fair but generous.

She remembered the emotion she'd seen in the eyes of the second taxi driver—that she'd misinterpreted as distress when surely it was gratitude. And she remembered, too, what Nabila had said about his modesty. And, understanding at last, her heart filled with pride and tears.

There was a silence, then Dexter glanced down at his watch. 'I ought to be getting back to the hospital pretty soon. I have a meeting with the planners about the extension.'

He paused and allowed another silence to fall between them, then he glanced across at her, his dark eyes narrowed. 'I've been thinking,' he said, 'about the pendant. I ought to have guessed the reason you'd taken it.' He held her gaze a moment and smiled ironically. 'But I'd forgotten what a low opinion you had of me. And since that was what you believed, you were right in what you did.' He smiled. 'I'll forgive you, if you'll forgive me.'

So, he believed her! That was wonderful! Harriet smiled delightedly. Then she narrowed her eyes at him. 'Forgive you for what?'

'For giving you such a scare.' Dexter threw her a wry glance. 'You went through hell those few days, carrying the ankh around in your bag. I knew that, but at the time I had no sympathy. Now I do and, as I said, I can only offer you my apologies.' The dark eyes twinkled. 'I hope you can forgive me?'

If he but knew it she would have forgiven him anything in the world! Harriet smiled into his face, her heart full of love for him, yet struggling to keep her heart from her eyes.

'I forgive you,' she answered. 'And anyway,' she added, 'if you believed I was trying to steal it, you were right to act the way you did.'

So all was forgiven between them. Harriet felt a bitter-sweet relief. But as an antidote to love, relief offered little comfort.

'So, what now?'

Harriet's heart fluttered as Dexter asked the question. Her eyebrows lifted. 'What do you mean, what now?'

'I mean about us. Where do we go from here?'

'From here?' All at once her heart was clattering inside her. She dropped her hands to her lap to hide their shaking. 'I don't know,' she answered. 'That's really up to you.'

'And you.' Dexter paused, letting his eyes drift over her. 'Perhaps, after what's happened, you no longer want to work for me? Perhaps you prefer to go ahead with the plans for your return?'

When she didn't answer immediately—all at once she was tongue-tied—he went on, 'Personally, I'd be grateful if you'd stay on. But, in the circumstances, I'm perfectly prepared to pay you in full whether you decide to go or stay.'

She could scarcely believe what he was saying. Harriet smiled with silly pleasure. 'I'd be more than happy to stay on.' Then she snatched her eyes away, suddenly embarrassed, once again fearing that she might have revealed herself too openly. 'I was really rather enjoying the work.'

'And you were doing a good job. I'd really like you to stay on.'

'In that case, I shall.'

Dexter nodded. 'So, it's settled.' He held her eyes with a smile, then glanced again at his watch. 'But now, I'm afraid, I really must be off. I'll see you tomorrow morning down in the lobby as usual.'

Then he rose to his feet and, leaving her there on the balcony, her heart singing with foolish pleasure inside, he turned on his heel and disappeared inside.

Harriet realised from the start that this would have to be handled carefully.

At all times, when she and Dexter were working together, she must remain in control of her emotions. She must never betray that she'd fallen in love with him. The commotion within her she must keep strictly to herself.

For she had no right to love him. He belonged to Nabila.

What she hadn't realised was how hard her task would prove to be. And Dexter, without realising it, was making it even harder.

The trouble was they had nothing left to fight about. There was no reason why, as well as being colleagues, they should not also now be friends. Clearly this, at least, was what Dexter believed. And it was this new informality between them that he seemed to be insisting on that Harriet found increasingly difficult to cope with.

'Why not come to the clinic with me this evening?' he suggested a couple of days later, as they were driving back from the tombs. 'I ought to be finished fairly early. We could have dinner afterwards.'

You and me and Nabila. How cosy, Harriet thought. She slanted him a look. She dared not look straight at him. The pain in her heart, she knew, was vivid in her eyes.

'I think I'd rather not... if you don't mind,' she answered formally. 'I'll just have an early dinner at the hotel, then go straight to bed.'

'Suit yourself.' His eyes were still on her. 'Don't you get a little fed up with dining alone every evening? I would have thought you'd welcome a bit of company.'

Harriet shook her head. 'I don't mind dining alone.'

What else could she say? Her heart was weeping. If he only knew how desperately she wanted to say yes, how she longed to spend more precious time in his company, even if she had to share him with Nabila.

But it was out of the question. When they were working in the caves they were always so busy that there was very little personal contact between them. But away from that environment, in the easy atmosphere of a restaurant, how would she be able to disguise her suffering or hide the hopeless yearning that seemed to fill her very soul?

No, it was impossible. She could not even think of it.

Feeling his eyes still on her, she turned quickly to glance at him, trying to force a casual smile, but knowing that she was failing. 'Believe me, I'm perfectly happy dining alone.'

Dexter said nothing for a moment. The dark eyes narrowed. Then he nodded and turned away. 'I understand,' he said.

What had that meant? Harriet wondered. What did he understand? But she did not ask. The subject was better dropped.

But then, a couple of days later, a strange incident occurred. One that was not so easily ignored.

As they disembarked from the ferry at the start of the day, as usual, they were met by Mohamed, their regular taxi driver. But he had someone with him—a young Egyptian—and as they approached the taxi he began to speak to Dexter in Arabic.

Dexter nodded. '*Tayyib.*' Then he turned to Harriet. 'This is Mohamed's friend. He's asking if it's OK if we give him a lift to one of the tombs. I have no objections, and I presume that you don't either?'

'Of course not.' Harriet shook her head. Little did she know she was soon to change her mind.

The trouble was that Dexter invited Mohamed's friend to sit in the front, while he climbed into the back beside Harriet. That ought not to have been a problem, but the back seat was small, and as he climbed in Dexter inadvertently brushed against her arm.

Her violent reaction would have been visible to a blind man. With a gasp, Harriet jerked away from him, as a charge of sensation, like live electricity, went shooting through her. The touch of him, the sudden warmth of him, pressing against her skin, was so sweet, yet so painful that tears sprang to her eyes.

He turned to look at her then, as she shrank back into the corner, her eyes averted, staring blindly through the window. And though he said nothing, it was clear her reaction had been noted.

By the time they reached the tomb, after dropping off Mohamed's friend, Harriet's agitation had increased rather than diminished. It was as though that small incident had knocked the lid off her control. All the emotions she had been holding in so tightly for so long suddenly seemed to be threatening to spill out into the open.

She climbed out of the taxi, her limbs leaden with the effort of holding on to what remained of her self-control. Then, like an automaton, she was following Dexter into the tomb, struggling to switch off the emotions that besieged her, suddenly horrified at the thought of being alone with him.

And that was why it happened. Her mind was not on what she was doing. As she stepped off the ramp that led across the entrance, all at once she missed her footing, stumbled and fell.

If she had been feeling less preoccupied, she would have risen to her feet instantly. But in her current emotionally befuddled state of mind, it took her a moment to gather herself together.

And it was in that moment that Dexter reached down to help her, offering her his hand to lift her to her feet. But as she glanced up to see him bending over her, the anxiety that gripped her suddenly tightened like a noose.

Abruptly, she drew away and tried to scramble to her feet unaided. But all that happened was that she slipped again. Her legs all at once had turned to paper.

'What the hell's the matter with you?'

Dexter bent down, grabbed hold of her and, before she could fend him off, lifted her like a rag doll to stand before him. His hands gripped her arms. He gave her a small shake. 'Come on, Harriet! What the devil's the matter?'

'I slipped. That's all.' In his grip she felt helpless. From head to toe she was trembling. Her eyes could barely focus.

'That's not what I'm talking about.' His gaze seared her with its heat. 'What I'm talking about is the way you're behaving with me. You're behaving as though I was some kind of leper!'

'What a ridiculous notion. I can't imagine where you got it from.' Harriet made a futile attempt to free herself—though, had she succeeded, she seriously doubted her ability to support herself. Her legs still felt as weak as a spider's.

Dexter continued to blaze down at her. 'You know very well what I'm talking about. Every time I come near you, you jump away from me. You can't even bear to look at me, it seems.'

'You're being silly.' She forced her eyes to fix on him. 'You're totally wrong. You're imagining things.'

'I wish I were.'

His grip on her had slackened. But he had not released her. He still held her firmly, though more gently than before. And there was an odd note in his voice as he spoke those four words, softly. And an even odder, heart-churning expression on his face.

Harriet could scarcely bear to look at him, yet could not tear her gaze away. She could feel her heart pumping with emotion inside her. And her eyes, she knew, were suddenly filled to overflowing with the uncontainable sense of misery that rose up inside her.

She sighed a small sigh, dropped her head, and closed her eyes. She felt like falling against him and letting the tears flow.

'Is it really so painful?' His breath ruffled her hair. The hands that were holding her had slipped around her waist. She could feel them, firm and warm and comforting.

Harriet glanced up, not quite certain what he had meant by that. As she frowned, shaking her head, unable to find an answer, he added softly, 'I wonder if this might help a little?'

Then he was gathering her against him, his arms embracing her, one hand in her hair, tilting her face to his. As a small moan escaped her lips, a soft moan of helpless longing, he sighed a shuddering sigh and bent to kiss her.

It was a kiss filled with gentleness and warmth and passion. It caused her heart to stand still and the blood to leap in her veins.

Harriet pressed against him, knowing it was wrong, yet unable to deny herself this small taste of heaven. Her arms twined around his neck, fingers tangling in his hair, loving its heavy, sleek, soft silkiness.

And, in that moment, if she had been offered all the gold in the world, she would not have found the strength within her to tear herself away from him.

'Sweet Harriet!'

His lips were hot and warm and soft, the whisper of his breath as sweet as honey against her cheek. As he continued to kiss her, and she to kiss him, the hunger he awakened tore like claws at her innards.

Oh, to feel those lips kiss every inch of her body! To feel those hands caress with love and passion every quivering dip and curve of her flesh! Such forbidden desires were like a torment to her soul.

He seemed in no hurry to release her. He kissed her again—her chin, her cheek, her nose, her hair. Then he drew back and gazed down at her, a dark look in his eyes.

'Oh, Harriet,' he murmured. 'What on earth are we to do with you?'

It was the flicker of compassion at the back of the dark eyes that caused Harriet to pull herself back from the edge of sanity. What was it he'd said? 'I wonder if this might help a little?' Had his kisses, she wondered in sudden horror, been intended as a kind of therapy?

He knows, she thought, and he's feeling sorry for me. He knows I love him, and this is an attempt to console me.

With a gasp of shame, she drew away. 'You don't have to do anything with me,' she told him indignantly. 'And certainly not that. That should never have happened.'

Dexter nodded and held her eyes. 'No. I suppose you're right. It should never have happened. And it won't happen again.'

He turned away abruptly. 'Let's get on with some work.'

Throughout the rest of the morning, it was as though nothing had ever happened. They worked together like the efficient team they had become, Dexter dictating notes and Harriet recording them and handing him instruments as he needed them.

But Harriet's heart felt heavy. Close to breaking. I can't go on like this. Not now, she kept telling herself. It had been hard enough trying to hide her love for him. Having to suffer his pity would be unbearable.

She waited until the morning's work was finished and they had driven in silence back to the hotel. In the lobby, Dexter turned to her. 'Will you be joining me for lunch?' The invitation sounded, at best, forced and half-hearted.

It was the perfect opening. Harriet shook her head. She looked him in the eye. 'No. I won't,' she answered. 'In fact,' she added, speaking the words quickly, afraid he might interrupt her or that she might lose courage, 'I think I ought to tell you I've come to a decision... I want to go back to England. As soon as possible. You said I had a choice, and that's what I've decided.'

She had expected some opposition, or at least an inquisition. He responded with neither. He simply nodded his head.

'I can't say I'm surprised. I've been half expecting that you would decide that.' He turned away and told her over his shoulder, 'This afternoon we'll go and fix up your ticket. You can probably leave tomorrow.'

The arrangements for Harriet's departure went ahead like clockwork. By that very same evening she had her ticket and a seat booked on the following afternoon's flight out of Luxor.

'I'm afraid I won't be able to see you off. I have things to do. But no doubt you'll manage on your own.'

Before he left for the hospital, after they'd returned from the travel agency, Dexter looked in on her as she sat at her word processor, transcribing the day's notes.

'And don't worry about reporting for work tomorrow morning.' As he spoke, he was already halfway out of the door again. He had barely even looked at her as he'd delivered his message. 'No doubt you'll have packing and stuff to do. I'll make out a cheque for you and leave it at Reception.'

Then the door closed and he was gone. Not even a goodbye. For a long time Harriet stared at the spot where he had been. I shall never see him again, she thought with a wrench of despair.

She turned back to her word processor and stared blankly at the keyboard. It was best this way. She knew it was best. What point would there have been in her hanging on here, growing more miserable and feeling more humiliated with each passing day?

And he knew too that it was best, though her departure was an inconvenience. That was why he hadn't tried to talk her into staying.

He probably also felt guilty for having kissed her—yesterday in the cave, and before, in the *calèche*. Though they had been meaningless kisses from his point of view, strictly speaking they should not have happened. He was engaged to Nabila and he was at heart a decent man. No doubt, on reflection, he'd regretted those kisses.

And me?

All at once, tears welled up inside her. I shall never regret them, she thought, meaningless though they were. And suddenly the thought that there would be no more kisses, no more Dexter, that he was gone from her life forever, felt like the closing of a heavy door.

Her body shook with a sob and tears spilled through her fingers as, with a cry of despair, she dropped her head into her hands and gave release at last to the dreadful howling anguish that seemed to tear her soul apart.

The taxi dropped her at Luxor airport in plenty of time.

Harriet climbed out, feeling in a kind of daze, yet filled with determination to put the past few weeks behind her. The future, that's what I must think of, she told herself determinedly. I must forget about all this and step back into my old life. That's what really matters. All this was just a dream.

As a porter took her bags and led her into the airport building, she forced herself to focus on her arrival back in England. The repairs to her dancing school would now be completed and in a couple of weeks' time the new term would begin.

She searched inside herself for the flare of excitement she knew she would normally have felt at this prospect. But it just wasn't there, she had to acknowledge bleakly. Not even a shadow. Not even a glimmer. Her heart felt like a dead thing lying inside her chest.

That will change. When I get back. She marched towards the check-in. Once I'm settled back into my normal environment I'll start to feel my old self again. I won't remember who Dexter Ross was!

She smiled wryly to herself. Nice try, she acknowledged. For she knew that, as enduringly as the pyramids, the memory of Dexter Ross was branded on her brain.

In no time at all her bags were checked in and she was heading towards the queue at Passport Control, the step that would finally put Luxor behind her. And it was at that precise moment that she was suddenly aware of a female voice calling, 'Harriet! Harriet!'

Harriet swung round in her tracks, her gaze flicking across the crowd. And then she saw them: Nabila and Dr Fahmy, waving and hurrying towards her.

'We couldn't let you go off without a final goodbye.' Nabila was a little breathless as she finally caught up with her. 'We couldn't let you leave Luxor without someone to wave you off.'

'That's terribly kind of you.'

Harriet felt moved by the gesture. After all, she scarcely knew Nabila. But there was something else apart from her feelings of gratitude that was suddenly impressing itself on her brain. Nabila and Dr Fahmy were quite openly holding hands!

'Too bad Dexter couldn't make it.' Dr Fahmy smiled regretfully. 'Apparently, he had urgent work to do at the tomb.'

'That was his story!' Nabila curled her nose. 'I love him dearly, and he is my cousin, but at times he can be as pigheaded as they come.' Then she shook her head, dismissing this tiresome problem, and turned her gentle gaze on Harriet. 'So, are you all ready for the——?'

But that was as far as she got. Harriet was cutting in. 'Excuse me... Did you say Dexter's your cousin?'

'Of course he is. Didn't you know that?' Nabila's dark eyes widened. 'Who on earth did you think he was?'

'I thought he was your boyfriend... Your fiancé,' Harriet amended. Suddenly her brain was doing cartwheels.

'My fiancé?' Nabila laughed. 'Ahmed's my fiancé!' She hugged Dr Fahmy's arm. 'This is the man I'm going to marry!'

Harriet was aware that her face had gone as white as paper. Her limbs had turned to water. Her stomach was churning. All at once nothing made any sense at all.

Nabila sensed her confusion. She reached out and touched her arm. 'Go ahead and tell me if it's none of my business ... but why are you leaving?' she asked in a soft voice.

Harriet flushed, feeling foolish, and glanced away in embarrassment. Because I love Dexter, was the simple answer. But she could not bring herself to say it. Instead, evasively, she answered, 'I thought he was engaged.'

There was a moment's silence, then Nabila moved closer. 'And do you know why he didn't come to see you off?'

'He said he had work to do...'

'That's utter nonsense. The reason he didn't come had nothing even remotely to do with work...' Nabila paused, then turned quickly to say something to Dr Fahmy in Arabic. Then, without further ado, as Ahmed Fahmy hurried off, she was guiding Harriet firmly towards the airport exit. 'Let's not waste any more time. I'll explain everything in the taxi.'

The next twenty minutes were a bewildering dream. Harriet was afraid to believe that any of it was really happening. For, suddenly, as Nabila took charge of the situation—assuring Harriet, 'Ahmed's gone to retrieve your bags'—they were heading for the ferry, and Harriet was listening to a tale she could never have thought up even in her wildest dreams.

And though more than anything in the world she wanted to believe it, Harriet's heart was still filled with fearful questions as they reached the ferry terminal and Nabila pushed her out.

'Go to him,' she commanded. 'You know where to find him.' Then she laughed. 'I have to go back to the airport now and pick up Ahmed and your bags.'

But, in spite of her fear, nothing could have stopped Harriet climbing aboard that ferry and heading for the West Bank. For now, suddenly, she was armed with the strongest of allies, that ally worth more than a battalion of armed troops...

For in her heart, uncertain still, but flickering bravely, was the bright, sustaining flame of hope.

CHAPTER TEN

By a stroke of pure chance, Mohamed, the taxi driver, was waiting at the other side of the river.

His face broke into a grin as soon as he saw her. '*Anisah* Harriet!' he exclaimed, throwing the car door open. '*T'fuddli!*' Please get in.

And then they were off, driving across the scorching desert, Harriet's heart tight within her, heading for the tomb.

As they drew up outside it, Harriet almost lost her nerve. Perhaps she should turn around and head back to the airport. She had missed her plane, but there would be another. For, if Nabila had been wrong, all that was destined to happen now was that she was about to make a resounding fool of herself!

But as she stepped out of the taxi, she was smiling in spite of her nervousness. Who cares? she thought recklessly. Sometimes you've got to take a chance. And if anything's worth taking a chance for, it has to be this!

She firmed her shoulders as the taxi turned around and headed back the way they had come. Here goes! she told herself, as she headed towards the cave.

It was as though he'd been expecting her. She had barely taken two steps when through the mouth of the cave stepped a tall dark-haired figure. And she felt her heart swell inside her and turn over at

the sight of him. Love and longing poured helplessly from her eyes.

As Dexter halted in his tracks, a frown creased
his brow. He looked down into her face. 'Am I
seeing things?'

Delight and apprehension mingled together inside
her. But the delight was stronger. A smile lit up
Harriet's face. I'm glad I came back, whatever
happens, she decided. Just to see him again is worth
any risk.

She shook her head. 'No, you're not seeing
things. I'm here because I have something to tell
you.'

'And what might that be?' He had come to stand
before her, his hands in his trouser pockets, the dark
eyes oddly cautious. 'It must be something pretty
important for you to have missed your flight.'

'It is important. At least, I think it is...' A
splutter of fear caused her smile to slip a little. It
was possible, after all, that he might not share her
opinion. He might consider her reason merely
foolish.

Suddenly nervous, Harriet amended her
statement slightly. 'What I mean is, it's just something I want to clear up.'

He had taken a step closer. 'So, go ahead. I'm
listening.' There was an intent look in his eyes, but
still they were cautious as he waited.

'It's about me.' Harriet's heart was racing inside
her. She had to gather all her courage to continue.
'Nabila told me you believed the reason I decided
to leave was because of my supposed continued attachment to my ex-fiancé. I just want you to
know...' She shrugged a little awkwardly. 'I just

want you to know nothing could be further from the truth.'

When he made no reply, but just continued to stare down at her, she added, 'I know you've always believed otherwise, but I've felt no attachment to Tom for a long time. I haven't even thought of him in weeks.'

She waited with bated breath for his reaction. Nabila had told her of his misconceptions about Tom, and that they were the reason he'd refused to see her off. Because he was angry. Angry and upset.

She'd found that hard to believe then and she found it hard to believe now, as, showing no reaction whatsoever, Dexter took another step towards her.

'Is that what you came to tell me?' he asked.

Harriet could scarcely bear to look at him. He was standing so close now she could feel the warm scent of him in her nostrils. She nodded soundlessly, giddy and afraid.

'So, why were you leaving? Tell me,' he demanded. 'If that wasn't the reason, there must have been some other.'

The very air around them seemed to hold its breath for a moment. Her answer, if she answered honestly, would inevitably be revealing. And suddenly the thought of revealing herself terrified Harriet. She felt her heart retreating. Perhaps Nabila had been wrong.

But Dexter was coming to her aid. One hand slipped round her waist. 'Tell me,' he urged her. 'Why did you decide to leave?'

Harriet's heart was shivering helplessly inside her. She paused a fraction of a second. Then she looked into his face. 'I thought,' she told him, 'that you and Nabila were engaged. That was why I decided to leave.'

Astonishment and disbelief collided on his face. He laughed out loud. 'You believed *what*? Good grief! What on earth made you believe a thing like that?'

'I saw you together and I could see that you were close.' She paused and added, just a touch accusingly, 'And you never thought to mention that you were cousins.'

'No, you're right, I didn't.' His expression sobered. 'It never occurred to me you might think that Nabila and I were involved. I'm not involved with anyone, my dear Harriet.' He paused and leaned back a little to look down into her face. 'At least, I wasn't until a few weeks ago.'

Harriet could not speak. She simply gazed up at him, at that face she adored and that now was gazing back at her with an expression she could not even dare to put a name to.

But then he bent towards her suddenly and kissed her forehead softly. 'What an idiot I've been. I got it all wrong. I really did believe you were still in love with your ex-fiancé.'

'I was never really in love with him.' Harriet's stomach was churning. 'I simply——'

But Dexter didn't care about that. He tugged her against him. 'All I want to know is that what you're telling me is true ... and that you came to find me for the reason I'm praying you came to find me ...'

He kissed her forehead again and held her softly for a moment. 'I love you,' he told her. 'With my heart and soul I love you.' Then he drew back, and with a frown looked into her eyes. 'Is it possible that you might love me?'

'It's a great deal more than possible.' Harriet reached up to touch his face, her heart suddenly alight with joy inside her. She stroked his puckered brow. 'I love you very much. That's the reason I came to find you.'

There was a moment of total silence as they stood there together, gazing into one another's eyes beneath the desert sun.

Then with a shout of joy Dexter embraced her, pulling her to him fiercely, crushing her against him. And she could feel all the love and longing inside him as he bent to kiss her waiting, smiling lips.

'There's only one more thing I want to know,' he murmured. 'Would you prefer to be married here or in England?'

They were married in London the following month, but six months later they were back in Luxor for the opening of the new wing of Zaynad Hospital— which Dexter had insisted on naming the Harriet Wing, after his new wife.

'Now the hospital bears the name of the two most important women in my life. The only two women I have ever truly loved.'

Harriet felt deeply honoured and moved by the compliment. Would she ever, she wondered, grow totally used to how wonderful her life had become with this man?

Her life had changed totally—though she still had her dancing school. Or, rather, she had two now—the original one in Sittingbourne, and the new one she had recently opened in central London.

But the focus of her life these days was Dexter. She found it impossible to imagine what her life had been like before him. And impossible, too, to recall how it had been in the days before her life was filled with so much love.

As she constantly reminded herself, she was the luckiest girl alive.

And now, at the end of the day's celebrations at the hospital, they were sitting on their hotel balcony sharing a bottle of champagne, while a thin silver crescent of moon shone high above them. The Prophet's eyebrow, Harriet thought, smiling happily.

'I have something for you.' Suddenly Dexter leaned towards her, reaching inside his pocket to draw out a small red velvet box. He handed it to Harriet. 'Open it,' he told her.

Harriet took the box. 'You're terrible!' she told him, laughing. 'You mustn't keep giving me presents all the time!'

He smiled back at her. 'And you mustn't keep trying to reform me! As I keep telling you, it's an utterly pointless exercise. I enjoy too much seeing the way your face lights up every time I give you something.'

'Like a child at Christmas?' Harriet felt her heart squeeze. Once, she had believed that he secretly mocked her for being so open with her emotions. Now she knew it was a part of her he had always found charming.

'I love your artlessness,' he'd told her. 'It's a wonderful and hard-to-come-by quality. Don't ever change,' he'd made her promise.

And now he was smiling as he sat beside her, watching her as she looked down at the red velvet box.

'Go on, open it,' he told her. 'This one's special.'

Harriet did as she was told. But, as she lifted the lid, suddenly her hands froze and her eyes flew open. She gasped out loud. 'I don't believe it! It's the ankh!'

Dexter threw her a teasing smile. 'Only a replica. The goldsmith sent it down from Cairo yesterday.' He rose to his feet and lifted the pendant, on its fine gold chain, carefully from the box. Then, bending over her, he fastened it round Harriet's neck.

'This is far too special to add to my collection. After all, in a way, that ankh brought us together.' He kissed the top of her head. 'I shall always be grateful to it.'

Harriet reached back and caught his hand and pressed it to her lips. She was suddenly so full of love for him that she could scarcely speak.

Then, very softly, she asked him, 'What was the name of that queen? The one who built the obelisk in honour of her husband.'

Dexter ruffled her hair. 'You mean the obelisk at Karnak Temple? That was none other than Queen Hatshepsut.'

Harriet rose to her feet and turned to face him, slipping her arms around his neck. 'You know, that night at the temple when you told me the story about how she wanted to build him an obelisk in gold, I envied her for having a man she could feel that way about.

'But I don't envy her any more.' She stood on tiptoe and kissed his lips. 'Now I, too, have a man I feel the same way about. If I could, Dexter Ross, I would build you a thousand obelisks, and every single one of them would be made of purest gold.'

'Does that mean you love me?' Dark eyes twinkled down at her.

'It means that I love you with all my soul.'

His arms slipped around her. He kissed her softly. 'In that case I have no need of golden obelisks. Your love is all my heart desires.'

And, as they looked into one another's eyes, their love spilling over, it seemed for a moment that, high above them in the sky, the Prophet's eyebrow lifted with a smile of approval.

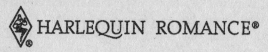 HARLEQUIN ROMANCE®

brings you

Stories that celebrate love, families and children!

Watch for our next Kids & Kisses title in November!

Who's Holding the Baby?
by Day Leclaire
Harlequin Romance #3338

Everybody loves this baby—but who's supposed to be looking after her? A delightful and very funny romance from the author of To Catch a Ghost *and* Once A Cowboy....

Toni's only three months old, and already she needs a scorecard to keep track of the people in her life! She's been temporarily left with her uncle Luc, who's recruited his secretary Grace, who's pretending to be his fiancée, hoping to mollify the police, who've called the child-welfare people, who believe that Grace and Luc are married! And then life starts to get *really* complicated....

Available wherever Harlequin books are sold.

EDGE OF ETERNITY
Jasmine Cresswell

Two years after their divorce, David Powell
and Eve Graham met again in Eternity,
Massachusetts—and this time there was magic
between them. But David was tied up in a
murder that no amount of small-town gossip
could free him from. When Eve was pulled into
the frenzy, he knew he had to come up with
some answers—including how to convince her
they should marry again...this time for keeps.

EDGE OF ETERNITY, available in
November from Intrigue, is the sixth book in
Harlequin's exciting new cross-line series,
WEDDINGS, INC.

Be sure to look for the final book, **VOWS,** by
Margaret Moore (Harlequin Historical #248),
coming in December.